"If you're **about pe**

"Of course I a ~~~~~~~~ ted irritably, glad of that excuse to refuse accomodation.

"Let them go to hell," Matt said. "What's more important? Can't you see the priorities?"

Eve's brain raced. If he treated her like a paid companion, and nothing else, that would be fine, however hurtful. But if he reached out for loving warmth...

"You forget, I'm well-known around here. I'm not having people think that I'm looking after your daughter by day and sleeping with you at night."

His eyes lingered on her body for a moment. "Now why should they think that?" he asked innocently.

Eve stared at him. Why indeed? Who could possibly imagine that this contained and sophisticated man would ever want an ordinary girl like her?

SARA WOOD lives in a rambling sixteenth-century home in the medieval town of Lewes amid the Sussex hills. Her sons have claimed the cellar for bikes, making ferret cages, taxidermy and winemaking, while Sara has virtually taken over the study with her reference books, word processor and what have you. Her amiable, tolerant husband, she says, squeezes in wherever he finds room. After having tried many careers—secretary, guest-house proprietor, play-group owner and primary teacher—she now finds writing romance novels gives her enormous pleasure.

Books by Sara Wood

HARLEQUIN PRESENTS
981—PASSION'S DAUGHTER

HARLEQUIN ROMANCE
2814—PERFUMES OF ARABIA

Don't miss any of our special offers. Write to us at the following address for information on our newest releases.

Harlequin Reader Service
901 Fuhrmann Blvd., P.O. Box 1397, Buffalo, NY 14240
Canadian address: P.O. Box 603,
Fort Erie, Ont. L2A 5X3

SARA WOOD

pure temptation

Harlequin Books

TORONTO • NEW YORK • LONDON
AMSTERDAM • PARIS • SYDNEY • HAMBURG
STOCKHOLM • ATHENS • TOKYO • MILAN

Harlequin Presents first edition April 1988
ISBN 0-373-11070-7

Original hardcover edition published in 1987
by Mills & Boon Limited

CHAPTER ONE

THE girl had run out of the velvet night and on to the floodlit terrace like a brightly skipping buttercup. She stood on the edge of the hotel's dance-terrace, her slender body delightedly responding to the samba's rhythm. The floor was deserted; it would be a while before the predominantly British guests lost their inhibitions and danced in the warm Mallorcan night.

Eve smiled at the girl's youth and vivacity, noticing how the buzz of conversation around her had changed in pitch and intensity.

'It's her!' whispered Jan.

'No!' Gavin, Jan's husband, stared hard.

'Where's the sugar-daddy then?' murmured Peter.

The smile on Eve's face faded in disappointment as her friends dissected the pretty girl, who was calling to a shadowy figure still climbing the broad limestone steps. A man, distinguishable only by a sliver of white shirt-front, had paused in the darkness. Oblivious to the fascinated gathering, the girl opened her arms to invite him to join her and gyrated saucily in perfect samba time.

'Oh gee,' murmured Gavin. 'Is that a pelmet she's wearing?'

'Pelmet?' answered Peter, his eyes fixed on the girl, 'All I can see is legs, legs and more legs.'

Eve glanced mildly at the two young men on either side of her. Their eyes were making a leisurely re-run, from the tiny gold strap shoes and the long baby-smooth legs,

to the brief apology of a canary-yellow dress, expertly cut
to leave the whole of her slender back quite naked.

'Not bad,' observed Gavin, with a low whistle.

'Not bad at all,' muttered his wife Jan, admiration
deepening her slight voice. 'What do you think, Eve?'

'Mmm?' Eve's head was on one side as she quietly
assessed the pretty flushed girl on the dance-floor. Such
fluffy blonde hair and riveting blue eyes! Yet there was
something in the girl's expression that caught Eve's
attention. It was almost as though she was terrified the
man would humiliate her by refusing to dance. How odd,
she mused. Now why was a saucy, confident girl so
unsure of her partner? Even if the rumours were true.
Usually, girls in *that* situation controlled the relationship.

'Trust you to be looking in the wrong direction. See
what the evening breeze blew in! You're missing one hell
of a man, Eve,' said Jan drily, seeing her friend was
studying the girl intently.

'Well, well, well, so *that's* what he looks like,' grinned
Peter.

The man had finally left the shadows, from where he
had been watching the girl. He made his entrance
slowly—it could only be called an 'entrance', since he
must have been aware that he was playing to an
audience. Could he know that his reputation had swept
through the hotel like wildfire? In measured, lithe
movements, he walked up to the pool of light on the
terrace, and stood surveying his hip-swinging partner.
Eve was astonished at the reaction of the women around
her. They had stiffened; sat straighter, with lifted chins,
assuming expressions ranging from sparkling excitement
to frank invitation. For the man was, without doubt,
sensational, and this was nothing to do with good looks.

If you analysed him, you'd come to the conclusion that you had seen more handsome men than he. His impact, however, came from the pure confidence of someone who rules his own world.

Compared to all other men there, he could have landed from another planet. For a start, his perfectly groomed city appearance was at odds with the casual holiday atmosphere. And, in the comfortable, middle-class hotel, his air of worldly sophistication immediately set him apart, and made it somehow acceptable to be staring, since that was what one did to such creatures, even if they weren't the subject of scandal.

His expensive hand-made suit—a dark charcoal two-piece—had been built around him, in long, painstaking and devoted fittings. It had been constructed to flatter the strong body beneath, allowing it to move with a graceful power that belied the subtle understatement of the elegant suiting. His veneer pretended glossy civilis-ation, elegant living, suave discussions in boardrooms and plenty of smooth-talking. Beneath, to the secret delight of the watching women, lay something entirely different: a man who had not lost any of the traits of his lusty ancestors. In an unconsciously nervous gesture, Eve patted smooth the neat knot of hair at the nape of her neck. He was evidently the kind of man who prompted women to check their appearances, thought Eve with a rueful smile at her own foolishness, even women as plain as she was.

For one ridiculous moment she wished she weren't wearing such a simple, cheap dress. She glanced down at the swirling pastel print, demurely exposing just a little of her lightly tanned chest, but giving no hint of her womanhood, other than its clinging, curving lines. Then, with an inner smile at such uncharacteristic vanity, she raised her thick-lashed eyes and surveyed the scene again.

'He is rather *mature* for her, isn't he?' whispered Jan.

It was difficult to place their ages. The girl couldn't have been much more than eighteen and he looked around thirty-five, though the golden light was kind and he might have been older. His neatly trimmed dark hair was streaked with silver at the temples and his face contained a world of laughter and sorrow. Fine lines radiated from the corners of his eyes, and harsh channels had been etched to scour deeply from his nose to the edges of his determined mouth. Not once had he glanced around; his expression of caution and watchfulness had rested continually on the buttercup girl.

He'd be interesting to talk to, Eve thought. He looked the kind of man who'd been places, experienced successes and defeats and come out on the winning side. Sadly, the most fascinating men never gave her a second glance; they didn't need her. It was the immature, the artless and those who had been dealt crushing blows by the world who flocked to her for solace.

She watched quietly as the girl blithely kicked off her sandals, which skittered close to their table. With a wry grin, the man strode across the floor and took possession of the girl's waist. The couple whirled around the floor, sparking off an atmosphere of tangible excitement and envy.

'More, more,' muttered Peter, enjoying the frequent display of smooth brown thigh.

'Some people,' said Gavin, 'have got no idea how to behave.'

But the man knew how to dance. He held his strong

body in a slightly curved tautness, his expression more
engrossed now and losing its brief smile. Caught up in
the fast Latin tempo, he concentrated on the steps,
dominating the happily flouncing girl with every turn of
his body and the firm pressure of his hands.

'Looks like he's going to shout "*Olé*" any minute,'
scoffed Peter.

Stealing a sideways glance at him, Eve wondered if he
was jealous. He and Gavin certainly seemed gauche
young men in comparison with the overtly masterful man
on the dance-floor. In all her twenty-six years, she had
never seen anyone with so much assurance.

'What nationality do you think he is, Eve?' wondered
Jan.

She considered. He might easily be a foreigner. That
darkness of skin *could* be a tan, of course, though to
achieve such a deep colour he must spend his winters
skiing and the rest of the year at Cap Ferrat, or wherever
the jet set hung out nowadays.

'Well?' prompted Jan.

'He's dressed like a European, but . . . I'm not sure he's
behaving much like one.'

For, as she pondered, he had been listening to the girl
very attentively, and then began to speak persuasively, as
if he was using all his considerable charm to get her to
change her mind about something. The girl's eyes were
locked with his, ignoring the sensual curl that appeared
at the corner of his mouth when he spoke. It was the way
it was shaped, Eve decided idly,—or maybe what he was
saying—that prompted such hints of devilry in his lips
and those wicked mocking eyes.

The band switched to a sultry rendering of 'L'Amour',
giving the Spanish crooner an opportunity to create a soft

world of romance for the guests. This was the kind of music that normally had them all flocking to dance in droves, but this time the floor-show was far too fascinating.

Earlier that afternoon, Liz Summer, the hotel's gossip, had spotted a devastatingly attractive man outside the local chemist shop.

'My dears,' she had shrieked to her two companions, '*who* is that gorgeous man?!'

A blonde teenager, purchasing sun-tan lotion and dressed—so the hotel guests were later told—in a poppy-coloured sarong, glared daggers at her and spat, 'That's my sugar-daddy. You keep off!'

Liz had gone on to describe the man in such detail that Jan had suggested she'd make a good police witness. And everyone had been on the lookout for the new arrivals, enjoying the added spice of intrigue to their holiday. So, for the moment, they were content to watch a real live outrage unfolding before their eyes.

Surprisingly, the couple weren't glued to each other during the sensual dance, holding each other's waists instead and talking, always talking. But he was so compellingly attractive that even the spread of his hands with the tips of his fingers in contact with the girl's naked back seemed suggestive.

'Isn't he sexy?' murmured Jan wistfully.

Eve frowned. 'I don't know how they can come here and flaunt their relationship so publicly,' she said quietly.

'He's not the sort to give a damn about anyone,' said Peter. 'She must be thrilled skinny to have such a super-charged lover. Besides, she's such a kid that she can hardly know what she's doing.'

The couple disturbed Eve's composure. It wasn't that

she was prudish about other people's morals—she lived and breathed Life's Drama at work, after all, and she never judged others by her own standards. But her own impression of the man confused her with its contradictions. He was too mature, too experienced in the world, to require some bolstering up of his approaching middle-age with an ingenue, however attractive. What would the two of them talk about? How could a man like that put up with the girl's inevitable unworldliness, however bubbly and stimulating she was? He must lack some moral fibre. What a shame. Another man falling short of her ideals. Maybe she expected too much. Her friends had said she was a bit too choosy.

'They've set the tongues wagging and no mistake,' marvelled Jan. 'They're almost like honeymooners.'

She was right. The couple showed a total lack of interest in their surroundings, paying exclusive attention to each other. If they had been honeymooners, that would have been charming, of course. As it was, the obvious sophistication, maturity and wealth of the man contrasted disgracefully with the youth and naïveté of his partner. There was a definite air of disapproval rippling through the soft night.

This wasn't exactly the wisest place to display an unconventional relationship, thought Eve wryly. The Molins Hotel, in the north of Mallorca, tended to attract mainly British holidaymakers, and had done so since it was first built and advertised exclusively in British brochures many years ago. The hotel's sedate and genteel clientele provided a safe and predictable environment for holidaymakers like Eve, who had to cope with enough dramas and unpredictability in her daily life without looking for them on holiday.

Sitting in their staid prints and sombre jackets, the guests were deeply scandalised by the strangers' blatant behaviour. Eve could sense the atmosphere stiffening around her, and by a little strategic wriggling in her chair saw that the couple were being discussed with some antagonism.

'Wish someone would be that wrapped up in me,' sighed Jan, eyeing the couple's oblivion to the rest of the world.

'Darling, I am,' answered Gavin, absently sliding an arm around her small shoulders. His eyes were still fixed on the long brown legs.

Eve smiled. Gavin adored his dainty, sparkling wife, she knew that, but there was no doubt that he had been temporarily distracted by the riveting effect of the couple, so flagrantly flaunting convention.

'Look how tenderly he's talking to her,' sighed Jan.

They were certainly affectionate, talking constantly, occasionally laughing together, sometimes frowning, worried, but all the time obviously caring and interested. Only lovers could have that much to say to one another. Eve relaxed into her chair, realising that she'd been leaning forwards, staring like everyone else. What did it matter if there was a huge age difference, if they were happy, after all? This was no ordinary wild passion, she had seen too many tender looks pass between them. If they loved one another, and fulfilled each other, it was no one's business but their own.

Her brow creased in thought. The girl seemed almost too bright, too alive, bubbling as though she could hardly contain her energy. Eve noticed that the man would occasionally take hold of her wrist with a warning glance in his eyes. He was over-tense; that tight-muscled posture owed more to reining in highly strung nerves than to arrogance. Strange.

'Come on, Eve, we'll dance too,' came Peter's voice.

'What?'

'You daydreamer! Trouble with you is, you're too placid. You'd be content to stay there watching everyone all night. I can't sit here alone with you and not ask you to dance. I've got my reputation to think of.'

She gave a gentle smile and slipped her tiny feet into her mules. She hadn't noticed that her friends were now dancing. Obediently, she took Peter's outstretched hand and followed him on to the floor.

Peter held her politely, not talking, and she gave herself to the dreamy, lovers' music, drifting gently as Peter swayed. Above, the night sky was shot through with tiny pinpricks of light. The sound of the surf on Cala San Vicente's rocks could be heard in the still warm night as the dark-eyed Spaniard sang softly of *l'amour*.

The floor was crowded, and Eve found herself barely shuffling around. Peter had drawn closer—not with any romantic intentions, Eve knew that, but because of the crush. He held her warmly curving body almost absently. She had met her friends here last year, before Gavin and Jan married, and they'd arranged to holiday at the same time again. They'd had such fun together, but it was all in friendship. Peter and Eve were friends, nothing else, with a common link in the type of work they did, since Peter was a Probation Officer. She had plenty of experience of them because of the students she taught. He certainly wasn't the kind of man she would entertain as a potential lover; he was a little too roving for her taste.

'No, I don't *want* to go to bed,' pouted a girlish voice behind her.

Eve's serious grey eyes lifted to Peter's face and saw his mouth was open. She fought to keep a straight face.

'But, my darling, I do.'

That voice was deep, rich and sultry. And English. It *must* be the wicked lover. Eve caught Peter's eye and he winked, manoeuvring them so that they stayed close to the couple. He was determined to listen and she shot him a reproving glance.

'I think you'd live in bed if you could,' sulked the girl.

Peter's hand gripped Eve's tightly and his eyes widened. An unaccountable sadness swept through Eve. How awful that he should be buying favours from a young girl.

'You're exaggerating as usual. Just please me,' said the man softly. 'Remember, I have needs as well as you.'

At that interesting point, the music changed to the second samba, sending all the British scuttling from the floor. For a moment, the couple stood motionless, talking. The man looked tired and slightly haggard, running one hand over his immaculate hair as if in exasperation. Then the girl reached up and kissed him gently on the cheek, a kind of pleading kiss. With a resigned shrug, he stepped back and swung automatically into the rhythm of the dance. Stranded, and too lacking in skill to do justice to the music, Peter and Eve made their way back to the table, where he recounted the conversation with gusto.

'The girl hasn't learnt there's a price to pay for being a kept woman,' grinned Gavin.

'Funny, I'd have thought he could have landed any

female rather than having to reach for the cradle,' mused Jan.

'What a peacock he is,' observed Peter. 'Those trousers are just a bit too tight for decency.'

'Hardly a peacock,' protested Jan. 'Plain dark suit, dazzling white shirt . . . I think it's the body underneath that's giving that impression. Can't you see those gorgeous chunks of legs?'

Eve could. The muscles bunched and flexed under the dark cloth and she found herself watching the fascinating strength of his thighs as he guided his partner. Her eyes flew to his equally powerful arms and the impressive width of his shoulders. Lucky girl.

'What are you thinking, Eve?' asked Gavin curiously. 'You've gone quite pink.'

Her startled gaze flickered sideways at him, then dropped demurely. She reached for her coffee-cup.

'Not bowled over by Lolita's lover, are you? I'd have thought you had more sense. Blasted man is strutting,' he complained. ''Tain't British.'

'Eve's head is screwed on far too tightly for it to be turned by a blackguard like that.' Peter ordered another round of café solos and brandies. 'I'm very suspicious of any man who can samba that well.'

'Good, isn't he?' breathed Jan.

'Very,' agreed Eve cautiously. The young girl was attempting to match his movements, but had none of his innate, carnal grace. From him radiated a powerful sexual energy; waves of it flowing out in all directions, reaching targets and zinging back. Eve was surprised to find that she, too, in common with the apparently disapproving women around, was strongly aware of his barely leashed passions.

Yet despite the apparent invitation of his body, Eve felt that he was not reacting to the girl, but was preoccupied in working out some inner devil of his own. With a shock, she registered the fact that he was now hardly conscious of his partner, and could have been dancing with anyone. He was lost in the music, using it to release some despair or restraint that had been controlled for too long, as if he had some violence that must find an outlet. The relationship didn't add up.

Discovering for herself that her partner was oblivious of her, the girl stopped and looked upset. It was a moment before he noticed and a wary, watchful look came into his eyes.

'Damn you, Matt!' she cried. She whirled around and stalked to a table.

'Looks like Matt is shelved for the night,' muttered Gavin.

'Rubbish! It's a game,' scoffed Jan. 'He's not bothered.'

Certainly he was standing quite casually, hands in pockets, flaring out the jacket at his hips. His expression was inscrutable. But for a fleeting moment, Eve had seen shutters sweep down over his face, the quickly clenched hands and sudden slump of his shoulders, as though he had temporarily succumbed to a bone-wearying emotional fatigue. Eve shuddered. It was all rather sordid.

Jan grabbed her arm. 'He's coming over here!' she stage-whispered.

Matt was looking for the gold sandals, and suddenly spotted them, still lying on the floor by their table. Ordinarily, one of Eve's group would have bent down and handed them to him, but they were too fascinated by the drama being played out to take their eyes off him for one moment.

The ankle-strap of one shoe had become looped under Peter's chair. Matt bent and wrestled with it, glancing up in surprise at the lack of co-operation, his eyes questioning, lingering on Peter, then on Gavin, sensing their hostility and scorn. Puzzled, he turned his head to Jan, who rewarded him with a melting smile and he recoiled, noticeably, killing all expression on his face. Finally, Eve was treated to a brief stare which grew longer to travel in some surprise over her light brown hair with its centre parting, every scrap of hair drawn back into a severe bun. Eve gulped in alarm. His gaze scanned her scrubbed face with its neat brows, straight nose and full, over-ripe lips. Awkwardly she shifted, trying to shake off his raking, all-seeing appraisal of her body under the mail-order dress.

She composed herself severely, and serenely met his eyes with her level grey ones, searching for his soul within and the key to his unease. His scything white teeth caught his lower lip and he dropped his eyes; but she had seen his troubled heart and something akin to desperation.

What was wrong?

Peter lifted his chair abruptly, releasing the shoe.

'Thank you,' said Matt sardonically, straightening up.

'Wow!' Jan gulped her brandy as Matt strode quickly back to his table, tapping the girl's nose gently with his forefinger in reproval and handing over the shoes with a smile that begged forgiveness, and received it.

The band had disappeared for refreshment, leaving a tape playing gentle Spanish music. In the warm night air the cicadas whirred their accompaniment, backed by the

booming sea. A hum of restrained murmurs buzzed on
the terrace as everyone discussed the shameless one-act
play they were being treated to. It seemed they all knew
where the second act would take place, despite the girl's
current fit of the sulks.

'Sugar-candy time,' grinned Gavin.

The girl was being handed a slender box, wrapped in
gold paper. She took it eagerly, her tantrum forgotten,
and tore at the wrapping. A small gasp went around the
terrace as she lifted out her present, her eyes glittering
with excitement. In the floodlight which skimmed their
table, a huge diamond necklace danced flashes of white
light from its kite-cut facets. Dangling like smooth pears,
six vulgar pendeloque stones hung at the centre, glowing
a cold ice-fire.

'Tacky,' muttered Peter.

'I should be so lucky,' grinned Jan.

'Oh, Jan,' said Eve. 'You've got Gavin.'

'Mmm. I s'pose I'll have to put up with what I've got,'
she grinned. 'Don't *you* fancy him, Eve?'

'Me? Why should I?'

'Dear old thing. Sometimes I wish I were as content
and undemanding of life as you.'

Eve smiled.

'Pelmet legs can't stop fingering her disgusting
present. His luck's in, I reckon.' Peter stretched out his
lanky legs.

'Peter!' Eve's gentle voice remonstrated mildly. 'Leave
the poor man alone. He's not happy.'

'Happy?' squawked Jan, as Matt fastened the necklace around the girl's neck and was rewarded by a girlish
hug. 'He's gorgeous, he's sexy, he's rolling in loot and he's
got a young dolly-bird. He'd be a fool not to be happy.'

Eve said nothing. There was something empty about those two; outwardly glitteringly beautiful, but inwardly both on edge, living on their nerves and, despite their apparent intimacy, acting like stangers tiptoeing around each other. For some reason, she felt sorry for them both, and then wondered at her impertinence.

'Eve's being her usual sweet self,' said Peter. 'Never judge, never think an unkind thought. Don't you get tired of being good? Ever considered a diet of iniquity and heinous abominations?'

'Once a month and twice on Mondays,' she retorted drily.

The spontaneous laughter from their table made everyone glance over at the lively young people. Attention focused on the quiet, graceful, mouse-haired woman, blushing furiously with lowered lashes. She appreciated the fact that any idea of her wickedness was hilarious to them. They knew the way she lived her life. As their laughter broke into helplessness, she began to smile broadly, then her face broke into a grin and finally she laughed too, a rare sight which lit her solemn face with its enchantment.

All evening she sat there, perfectly poised as always, an oasis of peace and tranquillity, while the others chatted around her. This was one of the best parts of her holidays here. She loved being with people, so long as she didn't become the centre of attention. Occasionally, in her grave thoughtful voice, she answered a question, or reluctantly gave an opinion, but for most of the time she contentedly watched her friends and listened.

Gradually, she became aware of a force drawing her eyes like a magnet, urging her to look up. Reluctantly she slowly lifted her eyes, knowing that there was only one person there who could have that effect. Directly opposite was Matt, and he was staring at her! It was an unusual enough experience to make her uncomfortable and disturb a little of her repose. He was alone now; slouched back lazily in his chair, seemingly at ease, elegant and nonchalant, watching her steadily. But the hands in his pockets were clenched again and the muscles of his face appeared to be under ruthless control. Eve considered him seriously, wondering what he found so interesting and why he was so tense.

Her head had tilted slightly to one side in earnest contemplation and her gentle eyes had widened in compassion, the generous arc of her upper lip parting to reveal neat pearly teeth. She sat, as always, upright and correct, unknowingly making the most of her full breasts which had been constrained in the simple dress. When she checked herself in mirrors, she saw nothing of this, only a very ordinary person, whose face was unremarkable, whose hair was an uninteresting colour, and whose body was rather top heavy. To others, she gave an impression of demure, unrealised womanhood, untouched by the materialistic world, the kind of woman who created her own atmosphere of peace wherever she went. And when she honoured anyone with a smile, or even one of her rare laughs, they felt privileged.

To her shock, Matt began to scan her body with greater intimacy and at greater leisure than before. Eve coloured hotly in discomfort. Men didn't look at her body. They looked at her eyes and their hearts poured out. She was good old Eve, den mother to hundreds, confidante and brow-soother.

The girl had reappeared from the direction of the hotel's powder-room, and Matt stood, his interest in Eve immediately eclipsed. He slid some notes from his wallet, tucked them under his glass and they left the dance-floor under the avid gaze of everyone there, disappearing into the dark night.

With their departure, Eve felt suddenly released from tension and strangely tired. It was as though her emotions had been held captive by the antics of the pair and now all that was left was an anti-climax. For a brief while, the scene had been lit by their sensational appearance, and it all seemed very drab now that they had gone. The evening stretched ahead with a sameness that she didn't relish. Peter would get a bit maudlin over the Spanish brandies and regale her with his life story once again, expecting a sympathetic ear. Jan would snuggle up to Gavin and tease him till he hauled her off to bed.

Normally she enjoyed their evenings. Now she felt a restlessness—and she did *not* want to watch Jan and Gavin become cheekily affectionate to one another. For once, she felt lonely; she, Eve, loved by everyone and loved by no one. Too many glasses of wine! she grumbled to herself.

'So that's where they sprang from,' cried Peter. 'Look!'

They followed his pointing finger and could just see a tall figure in an almost luminously white shirt, walking slowly up the steps of the large villa across the inlet.

Cala San Vicente was a remote and narrow cleft in ancient rocks, with a tiny golden beach at its head. The hotel was built on one side of the inlet, its rooms and terraces cascading geometrically down the hill to a final sunbathing area which offered palm-thatched shelters and loungers for the guests' comfort. Across the other side of the bay was a wilder peninsula, the final thrusting

rocks of a low sierra. When she first saw them, arching
stark vertical slices against the brilliant blue sky, Eve
thought their rugged tops looked as though they had been
nibbled by some giant child. Now, at night, their dense
blackness loomed menacingly, their bulk just visible
against the scattered stars.

Most of the terraced balconies of the hotel and the
huge picture windows of the dining-room faced across
the bay and looked directly towards a large ochre villa,
roofed with green arched tiles. Everyone at the Molins
admired it. Yet in all the three years that Eve had been
holidaying at the Cala, she had never seen anyone there.
It had been a dream of hers to explore it, to climb up from
the winding path, enter the arching gateway and clamber
up the terraces, to languish elegantly on the shaded patio.
She imagined herself under the palm-thatched pergola
that provided shade for a long dark table, large enough
for any extended family, laughing and talking over an
equally extended supper. There, on the dry-stone wall,
she would sit, framed against one of the huge terracotta
pots hung heavy with blood-red geraniums, sipping wine
with her adoring husband.

Now someone was destroying that dream; someone
unworthy to be in it!

Matt had stopped and his golden girl curved an arm
around his waist, there on the patio, where Eve had
imagined herself swinging dreamily in the sapphire-blue
hammock. After a brief conversation, they disappeared
indoors.

'Can't wait for episode two,' said Jan.

'You'll miss that. It's happening now,' grinned Peter.
'Who's for a walk round the hairpin bend to Betty's Bar?'

No doubt he was looking for female company. She

would leave him to it. 'Goodnight.' Eve rose quietly and smiled at the others.

'You go hunting on your own,' said Gavin. 'We'll walk up with Eve. We're turning in, too.' He reached for Jan and they cuddled into one another.

Eve felt something tear within her chest. Dangerous, envying others their love. She'd never done that before. How peculiar! Her tranquil self-sufficiency had been dented. Eve sighed, remembering that she was a born giver, not a receiver. She and her father both. He had always marvelled at how alike they were.

The feeling worsened when she bade a final goodnight to Gavin and Jan and made her way to the small single room at the side of the hotel. It would be nice, just for once, to have someone close—really close, someone of her own. Someone to confide in and share the simple, daily events of her life.

The heat hit her like a wall and she hastily switched on the air-conditioning, opening the balcony doors with a reckless disregard for mosquitoes. Her view embraced the little square and bars and at the back of the beach, the soaring scrub-covered hills and the small development of villas surrounded by sheltering umbrella pines. And she was exactly level with the ochre villa's patio.

Two upstairs windows threw yellow light on to the carved wooden balcony that ran the length of the upper storey. Briefly, the lights were blocked in turn as a figure opened each window and closed the green shutters. Both lights were extinguished and Eve felt inexplicably deserted by human life. Below her, around the dance-floor, people were still enjoying the soft night and the hum of their conversation trembled through the air like the sound of a distant hive. Small cafés at the back of the beach threw glowing, shafting light from under palm-thatched canopies where convivial groups sipped their drinks.

Eve puzzled over the sadness it aroused in her. Her life had been so fulfilled, so deeply content up to that night. She had everything, surely, that she wanted; a rewarding career, loving parents, just about enough money to be independent but not enough to corrupt her modest way of life. True, she still longed for romance, but had been prepared to wait until she met someone with values similar to her own. It hadn't bothered her that men found her rather dull and too sexually restrained for their taste. Several had even told her so. Her time would come. Somewhere in the world was the man for her; a man who held honour as dearly as she did.

She lay in her usual way, a neat, straight line, arms by her sides and with the single sheet pulled up to her chin. For some time, she thought about the girl in the canary-yellow dress. Strange, how different people could be. Yet for all their differences, most people wanted the same things in the end, love being the most essential. What kind of love did the girl have? Not one which offered security or constancy. Maybe that was why anguish lurked in both their eyes: they knew how transient their days together would be and they were desperate to make the most of them before the bubble burst.

The odd circumstances of their relationship gnawed away at her but she couldn't make sense of it, or the couple's behaviour. And it bothered her.

CHAPTER TWO

A STRONG wind had blown all night, rattling the balcony doors and whining around her room, high on the sixth floor. Eve was delighted when she pattered on to the balcony the next morning and saw huge breakers in the bay. She remembered the fun over the years before. Pedro the pedalo man was just raising the red danger flag, which streamed out in the wind, as stiff and flat as a board. He paid out a huge coil of rope and walked it across the beach to the rocks on the other side so that it hung just above the turmoil of great rollers which seethed up the narrow inlet.

After a very early, light breakfast, Eve hurried down to the beach, thrilled at the thundering, thrashing sea. No one was in the water yet. It was safe as far as the rope, and beyond that only fools would risk the cross-currents which swept backwards and forwards across the narrow bay. This was a dangerous coast when the seas raged like this, a coast where boats beat for shelter to safer havens. From a mirror-calm sea, conditions further out created such suddenly mountainous waves that occasionally boats would be caught in the inlet and dashed on to the rocks. Eve had heard of this from Pedro, who had lost two pedalos that year because he hadn't dragged them up the beach quickly enough.

She slipped her blue print dress over her head and folded it neatly just above her white pumps which were lined up carefully on the sand. Already the sun was hot and she stretched luxuriously in its rays, confident she

couldn't be seen from the hotel in the lee of the rock.
Adjusting the straps of her plain-cut one-piece, she
wriggled in the shimmering dark green lycra trying to
make her breasts a little less prominent, and wishing for
the umpteenth time that her hips weren't so full.

She ought to let her breakfast go down before she went
into the sea. For a few moments, she stood watching the
thunderous waves with pleasure, then leaned back on the
warm rock, unravelling the governess plait which had
been wound around her head and letting her hair fall in
unrestrained clouds around her shoulders. That morning
she had braided her hair while it was still a little damp
from the shower, and now it was released it dropped a
curtain of flattering Renaissance waves. Eve flicked
them back to fan over the rock above her head.

The sun seeped into her bones and she spread her body
indolently to receive the glorious heat on every inch of
skin. Eyes shut against the glare, she slid her straps down
over her shoulder and gave a huge sigh. This holiday was
costing an arm and a leg this year, but it was worth it,
even if she did have to live on bread and jam when she
returned!

Peace. Wonderful.

'Well, well, well. My dreams are fulfilled. Ever since I
was a snivelling boy, I always wanted to meet a stranded
mermaid. What do I do to ensure you don't return to the
Deep?'

Eve's eyes shot open and looked directly into a pair of
tawny gold-flecked lion's eyes. Matt's. Her first thought
was that he had, surely, never ever been a boy, let alone a
snivelling one! But in seconds, she was caught in the
mysteries of those amber-shot eyes and felt herself
swimming, out of her depth. Hastily she blotted out the
image, her thick lashes fluttering nervously on her

cheeks. Yet she was still acutely aware that he loomed over her, half naked, his hands either side of her arms in a presumptuous intimacy. She dared not raise herself; it would bring her right against his body.

'I don't suppose you'd like to practise a spot of luring on me?' he asked hopefully.

Her eyes shot open to find him grinning, his sensual mouth curving delightfully over teeth which gleamed like a neon light in contrast to his dark tan. Unable to help herself, she flicked a nervous glance down his bronzed body. As she did so, his broad chest expanded a little in response and he gave a low chuckle when her eyes reached his narrowing waist. In confusion, her lids dropped shyly, to shut even more tightly than before.

'A silent mermaid,' he observed, his voice indicating that he still smiled. 'Even better. And of course, you have no need to lure me. Here you are, and here I am. Perfect.'

Outrageous man! There was no question, of course, of giving him any reply. There was a presumption in his casual flirtation that made her stomach muscles tighten in anger, remembering as she did his strange infatuation for a girl half his age. He didn't speak again, but she knew he was still there, and his silence was unnerving, making her body tingle, alive to his presence. She lay still, feeling ridiculously exposed and vulnerable, knowing he was playing some kind of game or joke on her and refusing to be part of it. Yet an unholy tension was building up. Faintly, she heard the sound of his breathing, as though he had been running, and a delicate fan of air tantalised her face at intervals. Her own breath constricted in her throat and she swallowed in an effort to free herself from choking.

'I don't often get a chance to study a woman in such detail,' he murmured.

What was he doing? The sun on her lids burnt like fire as her body took up the flame and blushed under his wicked scrutiny. For a moment, his breath feathered deliciously over her upper chest, and she couldn't remain motionless any more, she had to dissipate the crackling suspension between them. Hesitantly, she risked glancing at him from under her lashes, only to discover that he was openly admiring her breasts! When she glanced down over her generous curves, she saw to her horror that she had stretched herself sufficiently to expose the first faint aureole of each strawberry nipple.

'*Oh!*' she moaned, grabbing the front of her costume and sitting up. That was a mistake: she was now virtually in his arms, the curling black hairs on his chest rasping her costume, his tanned face a breath away. The angle of his jaw fascinated Eve: never had she felt an irresistible urge to touch a man, but now she did. Her fingers itched to trace its lines and the sweep of his throat, to feel that smooth bronze skin. In confused distress she pressed her fingertips to the planes of his chest, withdrew them at the unnerving sensation and clutched at her heart in bewilderment. He stepped back, amused.

'Too close for comfort?' he asked softly.

'Take your attentions elsewhere,' she said in an oddly husky voice.

'I can't help my natural response to a pretty woman,' he murmured.

'I'm not pretty!'

He smiled at her surprise, his lips shaping into a devilishly appealing curve, just asking to be touched with ... Eve's eyes clouded in distress. Pulling her costume firmly into place, and flushing deeply with embarrassment, she ran past him into the sea, streams of hair bouncing in a frenzy of deceptively wicked waves.

Froths of white foam walled up in front of her as she surged up to the rope, hanging on to it tightly as the rollers lifted her off her feet and she cried aloud at the momentary fear and elation. Relief, too: relief to be at a distance from that awful man and at being able to release some of the pent-up feelings which had formed. She let out another low cry of shame and bewildered panic. Her response to this *unworthy* man was an utter mystery. She knew the kind of man she would find attractive, and Matt didn't come anywhere near that ideal.

A hand clapped down on top of hers and she looked up in shock, only to be taken unawares by the next wave which swept her right into his protecting arms. She felt the roundness of her own body, the soft yielding flesh, crushed against his unresisting hardness; felt his glistening, sliding wetness and warmth, then the sea subsided and she floated down to her feet again.

'What . . .?'

'I think you've lost your balance, mermaid.' His strong arms still held her.

She was unable to answer.

Another wave crashed into her defenceless body and his arms tightened. This time, she was aware of his smiling face, gazing down with those sinful eyes, his lashes thick with droplets, his hair streaming back from his broad forehead. Her gaze dropped in confusion, but encountered a daunting width of shoulder and the wet sheen of a smoothly contoured torso. In the swirling water, tiny hairs lifted and flattened against his chest in black curling slicks. He was beautiful.

'I'm not sure it's safe out here,' he muttered in her ear.

Eve wondered whether he was being intentionally ambiguous. Certainly the sea was a lot safer than he was! She made a valiant attempt to recover her composure and gravely pushed him away.

'I thought you were in trouble,' he protested.

'No!'

Thrown together yet again, they were swept into the bosom of the sea as it boiled around them, churning unexpected currents around their legs so that they hardly knew which way they'd be tossed next.

'Fun, isn't it?' yelled Matt, as they subsided once again.

Exhilarated by the wildly pounding surf, and by a strange wild sensation, Eve allowed a soft laugh to escape shockingly from her traitorous lips. For a moment, her eyes gleamed through the diamonds of water which dripped from her long crinkling hair. Matt's eyes narrowed, speculatively. Eve caught her breath at the power which surged from him, infusing her with wild ideas and dominating her body with its mastery.

Suddenly, she seemed to be surrounded by others, who were now diving into the surf and joining them on the rope. Safe at last! The waves dashed against her trembling body as she tried to reason that it was natural to be attracted to such a worldly, exotic man as this. He must be used to his power, even if she wasn't. Last night he had held women of all ages in the palm of his hand without even trying, and despite—or maybe because of—the scandal associated with him. Why should she be any different? But Eve didn't like it. She abhorred the warmth that had stolen into her body every time their bodies had touched and was appalled at his allure and her susceptibility.

'Damn,' muttered Matt. 'Where did all these people come from so suddenly? Just as it was getting wilder. Stormy, even. Do you recognise the signs of a tempest?'

'No.'

'There's a lot of turbulence,' he persisted, with a mocking smile.

Eve wished he would leave her alone. One of her friends might see her talking to him and that would be embarrassing, since he was the last man she wanted to be associated with.

In a massive surge from a giant wave, she was swept horizontally again and half drowned in spray. Matt struggled closer, hauling himself along the rope. Why wouldn't he take the hint? He couldn't be that insensitive.

'Oh!' she gasped, as her flesh made contact with his. A heat spread through her body in the chilled sea and she tried to disentangle herself, clutching at him, fighting to stop her legs from drifting up around his hips—and failing.

'Wonderful,' he whispered in her ear, the word creating warm gusts of air that tingled deliciously. 'I'm enjoying this.' His hands spanned her waist, the thumbs rotating slowly over her ribs, dangerously near to her breasts, which seemed to be fighting the constriction of her costume.

'Put me down!' she gasped, as her thighs slicked wetly around his waist. 'Put me down at once!' Her eyes flashed fear and fire.

'Certainly.'

It was the way he did it, of course. Eve had never imagined such a simple request could bring about such a complex reaction. First, he lifted her a little in the air, so that she was forced to place her hands on his broad shoulders for support. Somewhere in her stomach a hammer slammed hard, making her gasp. Her head shook in a frantic denial of the creeping trail of tingling nerves which were inexplicably taking over her body.

His eyes turned to liquid gold and the curve of his mouth deepened into raw sensuality.

'Down!' she croaked.

'Down,' he agreed.

And he slid her, slowly, languidly, right down his body, so that she felt the rock-hard muscle tensing against her yielding softness, and then when her pelvis was level with his, his relentless hands pulled her even closer with a shocking intimacy that she had never shared with any man before.

Her eyes glowed a molten lead, remote and frightened. He released her quietly.

'I thought you were in trouble there, for a moment,' he said gravely.

In panic, she drew back, frightened by the glow in his extraordinary eyes which had darkened to a honeyed caramel. Upset with herself, and deeply offended by his advances, she turned and forced her way through the surf, reaching the beach with relief. She picked up her towel and began to rub her body fiercely, as if to remove all evidence of his touch.

From her sun-lounger on the terrace, she stole occasional glances at him still enjoying the rough seas, leaping and diving into the pounding surf with an almost frantic energy. Eve puzzled over her encounter with him, wondering why he had flirted and why she had been so . . . disturbed. Well, they always said that nice girls fell for rakes, and that rakes found nice girls a challenge. Perhaps he was temporarily bored. Anger coursed through her body that he had made use of her in this way, causing such an unnerving reaction. *He* might be used to casual flirtations, but she certainly wasn't!

Mercifully, before Eve could dwell on the incident any more, various children and guests stopped to chat to her and she forgot him, particularly when one young woman began to pour out her troubles and ask for advice. The conversation continued over lunch at the beach-bar, and she listened earnestly, completely absorbed.

When Eve was sunbathing alone again that afternoon, the girl appeared on the beach and brought the Cala to pulsing life. Her name was soon known to everyone: Dodi. A name as abbreviated as the minute scraps of scarlet material, draped precariously over the vital parts of her anatomy. She wheedled a crowd of young people into a wild game of beachball, enticing most of the young men from the hotel beach terrace, leaving the old, the infirm, the jealous and the haters of boisterous games—like Eve—to watch the action.

And Matt. Throughout the teasing, the flirting, the squeals of false protest, he leaned in casual pretence against a rock at the edge of the sands, hands thrust deep into crisp white shorts, his brooding eyes constantly watching Dodi's exuberant antics.

Her behaviour shocked Eve. The age difference between Dodi and Matt had been tactlessly underlined. It was painful to watch, as Dodi teased the boys outrageously, but with such a vibrant appeal that it flooded the Cala with joy.

The boys had lost their patience and were holding her aloft, like a virgin to the sacrificial altar, bearing her in a solemn chanting procession to the crashing sea.

'A *one* . . . a *two* . . . a *threee*!'

Rather upset, Eve turned away from the scene, intending to read. But she caught the eyes of four hovering children, who bounded forwards at her responsive smile.

'Tell us a story like last time, Eve,' they begged.

Her stories had become a pleasure to the children in

the Cala, especially those who came year after year. Eve was always available, always willing and, as far as the adults were concerned, a very good influence.

As she invented a tale which included every one of the growing band of listeners in an improbably magical adventure, she became aware of Matt in the background. She paused to see his strained face. It couldn't have been easy, taking an unthinking teenager into his heart.

A fat little finger prodded her arm. 'Go on,' its owner urged. 'What did the croaking butterfly do next?'

'Yes,' murmured Matt. 'What *did* the ... er ... croaking butterfly do next?'

'It croaked,' said Eve sharply. 'Then ...' Her voice became conspiratorial and the children gathered closer, their eyes widening. Matt came nearer, too. Eve concentrated hard on the plot. At the end, when the magic lozenge had been fished up expertly by the children in a home-made net and the butterfly's voice was reduced to a civilised whisper again, the children begged for another story. Eve shooed them away, saying that her story batteries were flat and only sleep would charge them up.

'My dad joins his batteries up to someone else's,' said Little Fat Finger.

'What a jolly good idea,' exclaimed Matt, standing even closer to her chair. 'You children run away and I'll plug in immediately.'

An involuntary smile twitched at her lips. His soft breath whispered over her face, caressing it, and then, equally caressing, came his voice.

'You have quite a fan club. Can I join? Is there some intriguing method of entry?'

His words took her breath away.

'I forgot; you can't speak; flat batteries.' A strong

finger traced the shape of her rib cage. 'Need a spark or two?' he murmured.

He was quite without shame! Eve's distracted gaze dropped to his tanned legs, level with her eyes. The tautly muscled strong pillars disappeared into the brief white shorts that hugged his hips disgracefully. Today, he wore a knitted cotton T-shirt, equally clinging to the mounds of biceps and pectorals. She didn't want to talk to him while he was in this flirtatious mood. Squinting in the sun, she glared briefly at him.

'I'm trying to sleep,' she said pointedly.

'I wish I were as relaxed as you,' he growled, suddenly despondent. 'Do you mind if I sit with you a moment? I'm in urgent need of gentle female company. I'd like to talk to you, Eve . . .?'

'Foster,' she completed reluctantly. They came at her in droves, these people with troubles. His problem was easy to guess: how to keep his young mistress from straying. Eve frowned: his infatuation didn't make sense—he wasn't the sort. Could everyone be wrong? But then the girl had claimed him as her protector.

'You do an awful lot of thinking and not much talking,' he observed, squatting beside the lounger. 'I suppose it's lack of practice.'

He grinned at her puzzled look, the smile opening his face into an expression that dazzled her for a moment. 'Down there,' he said, waving a hand at the blue Mediterranean, 'where you mermaids live. Talking underwater would make the words sound bubbly. Tell me, do you go all squeaky when you go to great depths?'

Before she could stop herself, a treacherous laugh escaped her lips, then she stifled it. Great depths indeed! How could he look so innocent when he made that remark?

'You have the most delightful laugh I have ever heard,' said Matt. 'And the most stunning smile.'

He was beginning to unnerve her again. 'Please don't talk like that,' she murmured.

'Sorry. You make me nervous.'

'I do?' No one had ever said *that* to her before!

'Yes. I'm not sure . . .' He stopped and frowned.

Eve sighed, realising that he was finding it difficult to begin talking about his worries. A shout went up from the beach, where Dodi was chasing a young man who had taken the beachball. Matt half rose, then thought better of it, but his eyes followed the chase.

'You haven't introduced yourself,' she said hastily, trying to draw his mind in another direction. Scoundrel he might be, but she was usually able to help people by listening, and her heart had been softened by his plight, however self-induced it might be. She could never resist anyone in trouble. Maybe she could get him to see the potential disaster of such a relationship.

'Matt Cavell,' he said quietly. 'And you are the girl with the eyes.'

'I beg your pardon?'

'Fathomless dove-grey. I fell deeply into them last night when you tried to psychoanalyse me.'

'My apologies,' she said stiffly.

'It was flattering, though quite disconcerting.'

'You're staying at the villa?' she asked brightly.

'Mmmm.'

'Lucky you,' she said, desperate to take his mind off the girl.

'Mm.'

'Are you here just on holiday?' she enquired.

He shot her a suspicious glance and was reassured by the openness of her face. 'Sort of,' he answered shortly.

'You're renting the villa?'

His sombre eyes regarded her steadily. He knew what she was doing. 'It belongs to a friend I work with.'

'Oh! I've never seen anyone there before.'

'People in my line of business don't have much chance to take holidays.'

'What . . .'

'*Maaatt*!' The girl came haring along the terrace like a whirlwind. 'Darling, we're all gasping and I haven't brought any cash. Lend me some, there's a love.'

She gave Eve a broad smile and wriggled around the lounger to crouch between Matt's knees, pleading with bright eyes.

'Treating everyone, are you?' he asked drily.

'Everyone!' she agreed dramatically, spreading her arms to include the world.

With a wrench of his mouth, he slipped out his wallet. Her slender fingers delicately extracted some notes and she planted a smacking kiss on his cheek.

'Thanks a million,' she crowed. 'See you.'

In a flash of brown legs she was gone.

You do have problems, thought Eve. No wonder you're going grey.

'Talk to me,' he muttered, placing a cold hand on her knee.

In any other circumstances, she would have calmly removed his hand; for the moment, her compassion outweighed any affront she might have felt.

'What about?' she asked stupidly.

'Anything. Talk.'

An impossible request. She didn't chatter at the best of times. Aware of his glowering gaze at the raucous crowd around the bar, Eve cast around for inspiration and plunged in.

'Dodi——'

As soon as the word was out, she knew she had made a mistake. That's what came of talking before you thought.

'For heaven's sake!' He averted his gaze and stared out to sea. 'I want to hear about you.'

'Me? What on earth for?'

'Why not?' he countered.

A roar of laughter at the bar had Matt turning his head anxiously in that direction again. Eve was frightened by the simmering, barely controlled emotions which flooded his body and drove pain into his eyes. All he wanted was a distraction, any distraction. And she was concerned enough for him to comply.

'I've been coming here for years,' she began. 'People laugh at me, saying I'm unadventurous going to the same place every time. But I know what to expect and I love it here. I first came here as a child.'

She could visibly feel Matt shifting his mind, ready to hear her tale. Rarely did she open up to anyone; she was usually too busy listening to *them*. It suddenly became a roaring urge to tell him all about herself.

'I was five then,' she continued in her quiet, soothing voice.

'You came with your family?'

'Yes, mother, father and me. He'd had an unexpected bequest from a parishioner—he's a vicar, you know.'

'Ah. The picture is becoming clearer,' he said, smiling at her.

Good, she had his attention. In the background, she could hear the rumpus being caused by Dodi and gang, and turned her body towards him, fixing him with her clear grey eyes, and spoke even more softly so that he listened closely.

'Father would have spent the money on the parish—

the roof fund and so on. We tease him that the only bit of his brain that works is switched into Faith, Hope and Charity.'

'Not a bad condemnation,' said Matt.

'No,' agreed Eve. 'He's a darling. Everyone adores him. The biggest compliment people can pay me is to say how alike we are.' Her eyes were dreamy.

'Then you must be a very unusual woman to find that a compliment,' murmured Matt in a low voice.

'Oh, if you knew him, you'd understand,' she said. A sudden image of her plump-faced father, welcoming Matt to the rambling old Edwardian vicarage, suddenly shot through her brain.

'I'll make do with the daughter,' answered Matt.

'You're putting me off my story,' said Eve.

He smiled darkly. 'Your father was frittering money away on a roof fund.'

Eve's laugh tinkled out and Matt relaxed even more.

'He'd have a fit to hear you say such a thing,' she reproved with a grin. 'It was Mother, actually, who eventually persuaded Father that it was beneficial to his flock in the end, if he returned refreshed and ready for more good works.'

'Look, Eve, look at my fish!' squealed a tiny voice.

A little girl was nudging her arm and waving a yellow bucket under her nose. Eve gravely admired the minuscule rainbow creature, swimming frantically in the water.

'Isn't it lovely! Look how the scales shine, as if they're mirrors! Can you see your face?' The two of them peered at the fish, their heads touching.

'I saw me,' said the child solemnly. 'Did you see you?'

'Definitely. You'll put it back in the sea when you've shown Mummy and Daddy, won't you,' urged Eve.

'Yup. I'm goin' to catch a shark next.'

'What about a mermaid?' enquired Matt, dead-pan.
The child's face showed scorn. 'You don't catch
mermaids, silly,' she said scathingly. 'They catch *you*.
Sharks is much more dangerous.'

'Oh, I don't know,' murmured Matt.

''Course they are. You wouldn't find a shark with
combs and mirrors and silly hair. He doesn't know much,
does he, Eve? I'll show you my shark when I get it.'

Eve and Matt watched the girl leave, carrying her
precious bucket very carefully so that the water didn't
slop out.

'I shall have an abiding vision of a shark with long
golden hair, sitting on some rock far out to sea and
admiring itself in a hand-mirror,' grinned Matt. 'That
little mite certainly put me in my place,' he continued, to
Eve's gurgle of laughter.

'She didn't fall for your charm, did she?' taunted Eve,
amused at his rueful face.

'Will you?' he asked, suddenly serious.

CHAPTER THREE

THE silence hung between them, unbreakable for a few eternal seconds. It would be so easy to be one of the legion of women who must have fallen at his feet, helpless against the driving, animal magnetism. But Eve was made of sterner stuff: she looked for deeper qualities in a man.

'Of course not,' she answered shakily.

'Pity.' Matt eased himself into a more comfortable position and watched as she exchanged pleasantries with a passing couple. 'Everyone here seems to know you. I suppose you must know the area well by now, after all these years,' he remarked.

Inwardly relieved that he had accepted her mild refusal without question, she relaxed, determined to make her conversation appear quite normal. 'Oh, we didn't return after that first visit. The memory of that holiday lived on, fuelled by a bulging photo album. We had no more holidays because we moved from Cornwall to busy Brighton, and there was simply no time for a break.'

Matt stretched out full-length on his back in the sun, tilting back his head and closing his eyes. As his extraordinarily long lashes fluttered silkily on his cheeks, Eve was able to study his body without fear of being seen. He was relaxing all his muscles consciously. She could see him going through them, one by one. She had never watched a man's body so attentively before and was fascinated in the way the muscles flexed and relaxed under the bronze skin.

'When *did* you return?' he asked lazily.

'I've been coming here for the last three years. It does rather break my piggy-bank, but it's worth it. It's a real rest from being so much in demand.'

'Ah. The boyfriends.'

'Good heavens, no! I . . . I don't really match up to men's idea of a good time,' she said, her eyes lowered.

He smiled. 'One special man, maybe?'

'Nnno.'

One eye opened and quizzed her. 'None? Is that because you refuse not only my advances but everyone else's as well?'

She blushed. Her relationships weren't for public discussion. 'I'm not very sociable.'

'That's not true. You're very popular. Everyone seems to smile or wave at you. Hordes of children keep invading your privacy.'

'That's different,' said Eve suddenly breathless that he had followed her movements so closely. 'I like people. I'm not keen on . . .' Her voice tailed off. She was talking too much.

'Don't tell me you don't like men,' he murmured.

'Um, to be honest, I don't find them very interesting. Not interesting enough to use up an evening, anyway.'

'Condemned,' he intoned. 'Not worth a few measly hours of your time . . .'

'Oh dear, you make me sound arrogant. It's not like that. I can't explain . . .' She had got into deep water.

'Try.'

Darn it! Eve thought hard. 'There seems to be a kind of ritual, a way of approach and a path that men and women are supposed to follow. I just find it all rather contrived.'

'It can be fun,' he said, raising himself on one elbow.

'Maybe. At the moment my work is more urgent. A lot of my evenings tend to become an extension of my working day. People have problems and ring me up. I'm the original listener.'

'You're talking to me.'

That's because you need it, she thought. You need someone droning on, obliterating what your paramour is up to. 'Well, I'm entitled, it's my holiday,' she said with mock haughtiness.

Matt sat up, his face suddenly close to hers. She was about to pull back in confusion, unwilling to accept such nearness, but he caught her head in his hands and examined her face solemnly.

'I'm trying to decide what your job is,' he said.

'You won't find any clues like that,' she answered huskily, wishing for release from the tight pressure in her chest.

He grinned, and for one mad moment she wanted to feel those sharp white teeth nipping her flesh. Heavens! The man was related to the devil!

'You're a nurse,' he said finally, then frowned. 'No. You're not brisk enough. The patients would walk all over you. I can't think of a suitable job, where you could use your talents.'

'My talents?' Her soft brows rose in amusement.

'Tranquillity. Being with you is like lying in a silken sea, floating weightlessly, gently supported but not crushed. Being accepted but not absorbed.' Matt's eyes had softened meltingly into a tawny gold, his lids partly closed in . . . desire? Eve found her heart beating faster as his lips became fuller before her hypnotised eyes.

'Do you know, I'm relaxing for the first time in years,' he continued. 'I know that's partly because I've never had such a long break without problems of work interrupting, but I have the oddest sensation that I have all the time in the world ahead of me. It's a great feeling. Part of it is a response to what is emanating from you. I'm not sure what it is, but it warms me inside.'

Someone's tea-tray rattled behind Eve. She reached up and firmly drew away his hands and sought safety in practicalities. 'You asked about my job. I teach in a Technical College.'

'Teach! I'd never have thought that. So, what vital knowledge are you imparting to future generations?'

Eve forced herself to concentrate on thinking about her unruly group back home. 'Life-skills. I run all the Youth courses and also teach a group of ten supposedly ineducable teenagers.'

'Do you indeed? Now that's very interesting. Tell me more.'

Eve was flattered. 'They learn how to get on with each other, how to cope with each other's problems, how to write a letter, go for an interview, express themselves . . .'

Eve's voice became intense as she continued. Matt drew closer, watching her suddenly animated face and wondering at the changing patterns of care, tenderness and anger there.

'We take small steps at a time so they're constantly successful. They have a lot of difficulties and I never know what's going to happen when I walk in each morning, or what is likely to happen the next minute. Their backgrounds are so unstable, usually, and something at home can cause unpredictable and violent behaviour at college.'

'You're remarkable,' said Matt in admiration.

'Oh, no. I just do the job,' said Eve modestly. 'I've been so lucky, you see, with my home life. It would be a shame if I couldn't help less fortunate people in a positive way.'

'Do you find them work?'

'First I try to give them a chance to experience what it's like to enjoy a satisfying day's work without the pressures and anxieties of being employed. I arrange work experiences, using the local craftsmen, shop-keepers and so on. Of course, it means I have to twist their arms a bit, but I have lots on my books now, bricklayers, carpenters, plumbers, electricians, hair-dressers and so on. They often move into the same kind of employment. If not, we find something that does suit them eventually. There's one lad in my group, complete with dangling earrings and studded leathers and bovver-boots, who seems to have grown a ghetto blaster on his shoulder. Well, he's a whizz at hair-styling. I can't tell you what pleasure it gives me, seeing these surly, dull-eyed teenagers gathering confidence . . .' Her voice faltered in confusion.

'Go on,' he said softly.

'I've never talked so much in my life!'

'Really?'

The look in his eyes thrust stabs of fire into her body. She clutched herself protectively. 'No. I'm afraid I'm boring you.'

'Not at all. Anyone who can work with teenagers has my utmost admiration and interest.'

Of course, she thought with an odd sensation of disappointment. She should have realised, he wasn't interested in *her*, only as a means to an end.

'Look, let me order some tea and cakes. I'd like to hear more,' he said with a gentle smile.

'No, thank you,' she said, a little primly. 'I have to watch my figure.'

'How about a compromise? You eat and I'll watch it.'

'I never eat between meals,' she said desperately, trying not to enjoy his flirtation.

'That's boring,' laughed Matt.

'I'd be even fatter than I am if I did.' Eve was always painfully aware of her too-fleshy body. All around, aerobic-honed bodies mocked her with their tight, firm muscles, while she seemed incapable of re-shaping her curves.

'You're built like a true woman, thank heavens,' said Matt, dismissing the firm-bodied women who were parading rather obviously near him. 'Now. About that tea. Can't I tempt you?'

His teasing eyes and mouth were very close and Eve's throat constricted. She ran the tip of her tongue nervously over her lips, but paused in mid-action at the expression on his face.

'Hell!' he muttered, almost to himself. 'What are you doing to me, woman?'

'Please! Leave me alone!'

'I'm not sure I can,' he said slowly. 'You're very stimulating, and yet restful to be with.'

'So everyone tells me,' she said with unaccustomed irritation. This conversation hadn't taken the turn she'd expected. Now she was even more confused about his attitude and morals—and just what he wanted from her.

She was soon to find out.

'You are very rich,' he said, his warm voice making the hairs on the back of her neck prickle with the underlying sensuality. 'Serene, self-sufficient and fulfilled. I need someone like you, Eve.'

'Wwwwhat?' she gasped. A flood of anger curled in her veins, startling her. So, he needed someone like her! That darned aunty role again! He wanted a friendly ear; well, she resented that, though for the life of her she didn't understand why—she had decided to talk to him on that basis, after all!

'Oh! Look at the time!' she cried, examining her watch with feigned surprise. 'I must go. Excuse me.'

'You won't always be able to run away from me,' he murmured, amusement dancing in his eyes.

'I don't know what you mean,' she said nervously, gathering her belongings and thrusting them into her beach bag, her legs trembling inexplicably.

As she walked away, she knew that he followed every step. Awkwardly, she twitched down the plainly cut costume, ensuring it fitted snugly around the tops of her legs. There was a low chuckle. She turned, the fire of her anger reaching from deep within and spreading over her pale-gold skin. Matt raised one eyebrow roguishly and gave her an unabashed grin, then kissed his fingertips to her.

He really was the most infuriating man! With a skill born of long practice, he had flattered her with every intention of getting her advice about Dodi. It was all perfectly obvious and she was furious with herself for finding him amusing and attractive. So rarely did any man try to make her laugh ...

That evening she excused herself from the crowd who had drifted on to the terrace for after-dinner coffee. She wanted peace. Things were getting a bit out of hand. All through dinner, her friends had speculated about Matt and tried to prise from Eve whether or not he had let any interesting bits of gossip slip during their conversation. They wouldn't believe her when she said she had done all the talking.

She crept into the cool, marble-floored lounge which was rarely used, and curled up in a comfortable armchair to read. The words blurred. Eve shut the book and stared into space. If only Matt would extricate himself from his entanglement! It was obvious he and Dodi cared for each other, but it was a ridiculous situation.

'Hello.'

Eve looked up. A strangely demure Dodi had pattered in, dressed in a collarbone-grazing white dress, with slatted shoulders and a fitting bodice which swirled into a graceful skirt. Her bare feet twiddled on the cold marble. Despite its simplicity, the dress flattered her in a way that Eve's plain smoky-grey dress never could. Without envy, she admired the slenderness of the girl's body, comparing it with her own generous figure.

'You're Eve, aren't you?' Dodi's fingers twisted in unison with her feet. 'Matt was talking about you earlier.'

'Was he?' said Eve drily. Then, as the girl came closer, she saw the tell-tale blotchy face and still unshed tears.

'Did . . . did he say anything about me?' asked Dodi anxiously.

'No, he didn't.'

'He was with you while I was on the beach—are you *sure* he didn't make any remarks?'

Eve shook her head. 'None,' she said gently.

Poor girl! She looked very cowed.

Dodi came forwards in a rush and sank to the ground at Eve's feet. 'He's awfully mad with me. He thinks I was making an exhibition of myself. He's awfully strict, don't

you think? I wasn't behaving badly, was I? He said you'd
worked with people of my age. Please say I wasn't being
provocative!'

So he'd read the riot act to her! Quite the wrong thing
to do. 'It's all right, Dodi,' said Eve softly, touching the
baby curls.

'No, it's not,' she wailed. 'I wish it was. I was only
having fun. I can't seem to judge whether . . .'

To Eve's horror, tiny tears squeezed from the corners
of the girl's eyes.

'My dear girl, don't cry, it's nothing to cry about.'

'You don't understand! He said some awful things!'
sobbed Dodi. 'He's been lecturing me for hours. Now
he's gone all cold on me. Eve, I can't bear his distaste. I
feel a worm! I don't think he'll ever love me again and I
couldn't stand that! I need him badly!'

'Poor child,' crooned Eve, reaching out her arms.

Dodi curled into their shelter and sobbed her heart out
in great heaving gusts of breath. Eve let the girl tire
herself, then set to with a handkerchief to repair some of
the damage. She was concerned with the depth of feeling
that the girl was showing for Matt. It wasn't natural. She
seemed obsessed.

'What can I do to make him love me again?' asked
Dodi pathetically.

'Well, you can't ever *make* someone love you,' said Eve
slowly, 'but you can try to adapt a little to their ways. It's
very difficult making a relationship work sometimes,
people are bound to have differences, that's human
nature.'

'He's all I have,' she said.

'I see.'

'If he throws me out, I'll have to go back to England

and live in the Home ... Oh, *damn!*'

'What?' Eve tipped up the girl's face and stared hard at her. Tear-stained, she looked younger than she had first imagined. 'Just how old are you?' she asked severely.

'Eighteen.' Dodie wouldn't meet Eve's eyes, then was forced to. 'Well ... seventeen.'

Eve's eyes rounded and her lips parted in horror.

'Don't tell!' cried Dodi. 'They made me a Ward of Court, you see. Matt fought for me, but they said no, I hadn't known him long enough and they thought I needed protection.' She was gabbling in her anxiety.

'You hadn't known him long ... You were in care ...' What was the world coming to? Eve knew that social workers were more permissive now, but it was unthinkable that they should have even contemplated the idea of putting Dodi under Matt's protection.

'You don't have any family of your own?' asked Eve.

'All I have is Matt.'

'So was it because of him that they made you a Ward of Court?'

'Yes. No, not exactly.' Dodi began to twist the material of Eve's dress into rags, her eyes darting spasmodically. 'It ... it was ... I can't say,' she whispered.

'Wouldn't it help if you did?'

'*No!*' The word was bitten out with such force that Eve started back. The child had withdrawn, her hands shaking, retreating into some private horror. The pupils of her eyes were tiny pinpricks of black.

'Poor Dodi,' soothed Eve, gathering the girl to her bosom again.

'All I want to do is please him. He's upset when I'm

depressed, then worries when I lark around. I never seem to get things right. Do you think he's just being nice sometimes because he has to?'

What an extraordinary question, thought Eve! And how could she answer? She ought to discourage the girl, for her own sake.

Matt's voice rescued her from her predicament.

'No, he's not being nice out of duty,' he answered tenderly. 'Come here, you idiot girl.'

'Oh, Matt!' Radiant, Dodi ran into his arms and was swirled around into the air.

'I love you very much. You know why I worry,' he said quietly.

'I do, I do! And I see what you meant when you said I ought to be more like Eve.'

Hearing this, Eve was aghast. How could he crush the poor girl with such a tactless remark?

'Then you show remarkable sense after all,' said Matt approvingly. 'Now off you go. I want to talk to her.'

'Yes, Matt,' Dodi said obediently.

When she had gone, his body suddenly tensed and the lines on his face deepened.

'I'm not sure I can cope,' he muttered. 'Keeping an eye on that girl and her morals is more difficult than I ever imagined. I have no yardstick; teenagers are a mystery to me.'

Eve gazed at his dark head and the black hair which curved so neatly on his tanned neck. The width of his shoulders was emphasised by the tailored linen jacket, and vague stirrings tightened Eve's chest which she interpreted as sympathy.

'I'm sorry you're mixed up in this,' he continued.

'I'm sorry too,' she replied coolly.

'What has she told you?' His expression was guarded.

In her usual way, she thought first of the impact of her words and decided to give it to him straight. 'That she wants desperately to please you, that she's only seventeen and a Ward of Court.'

Her steady eyes watched his reaction. He groaned and closed his eyes in pain. 'If you tell anyone that, then everything I've done over the last couple of weeks will be for nothing. You'll destroy her. God! If you could have seen her when I picked her up! I tell you, she was a mad, desperate creature.'

So the child was just a casual pick-up then, swept by this man into a maelstrom of emotion, too complicated for her to handle. But how and where had he met her?

'I rarely give direct advice,' she said slowly. 'But I think you should give her up.'

'*No*! Who else would she turn to? I love her!'

'Sometimes love means being unselfish and thinking of the other person.'

'But she needs me!'

'You've made her need you!' cried Eve angrily. 'You could have left her alone! You're supposed to be a mature, reasoning adult. The responsibility is yours.'

Matt's white teeth tore into his lower lip. 'You can't think that I should have left her in the Home. My instincts . . .'

'Your instincts were blurred by your own needs,' scorned Eve, furious that he had been so blind.

'No!' He shook his head in denial, agony etched in every line of his face.

'Of course they were. If you'd thought of her welfare for one moment, you would have seen that what you were doing was unforgivable. You admit you know nothing about girls of her age: they're vulnerable, however confident they may seem on the surface. You should have left her with experts.'

'Experts!' he exploded. 'She was going through hell. I had to get her away.'

Eve was startled at the extent of his passion; this man felt very deeply, cared with intensity. His anger, now directed at her, threatened to become physical—she could see how he could barely contain himself in the way his hands clenched and the muscles of his body were tensing, ready to attack. But she had to speak her mind. What he was doing was wrong, and despite the fact that she usually manoeuvred people to make up their own minds about problems, she couldn't let this relationship go on any longer.

'It didn't have to be you who gave her shelter. Surely you can see she ought to be with foster parents? The girl needs a mother and a father.'

'Dammit! What the hell do you think I was doing? Are you saying a stranger would make a better father than me? She's my child, I care for her more than anyone!' he yelled back, his eyes flashing fury.

'Your . . . *what* did you say? Dodi's not your daughter.'

'Of course she is! What else?' He saw her horrified face and strode quickly to her, his hands seeming to crush the bones of her shoulders. 'Just what did you think?' he asked savagely.

'You're hurting! Please! I . . . oh, this is awful! I thought—everybody thought that you and she were lovers!'

Matt gasped in shock and his hands fell away abruptly. 'Everybody? Why? What on earth gave them that idea?' he demanded.

'Dodi told a woman that you were her sugar-daddy,' said Eve weakly.

'God! The little minx! Was this woman by any chance making remarks about me at the time?' he asked shrewdly.

Eve nodded. 'She indicated that she fancied you.'

Matt heaved a sigh. 'Poor kid. Every time she thinks a woman is taking an interest, she scares them away. She wants my undivided attention.'

'But I heard . . .' Eve blushed, then plunged on. She had to know. 'You were talking about going to bed and having needs,' she said in acute embarrassment.

'Damn right. I'd spent the previous two nights in an armchair in her hotel-room because she was afraid of being alone,' he growled. 'Anything else?'

'Well . . . you gave her an expensive necklace . . .'

'Good God! You've all been adding up everything I've done! Haven't you anything better to do? The necklace was my wife's and Dodi always loved it. Ugly, pretentious piece! The necklace, I mean. My wife was never ugly.'

His teeth caught his lower lip again, and the look of anguish as he spoke of his beautiful wife evoked a spear of echoing pain that swept through Eve's body, leaving her strangely sad.

'Oh,' she said in a small voice. 'I'm sorry. It all seemed to make sense, though somehow I knew you weren't the kind of man to . . . to . . .' She faltered at his penetrating gaze.

'Hell, what a mess!' he exclaimed. 'Let me explain a little.'

'If you think it will help.' Eve deliberately kept her voice calm and unemotional.

'It will—me, if not you or Dodi,' said Matt grimly, drawing Eve to the sofa. She sat nervously near him, her hands quite still in her lap, despite the urge to reach over and smooth out those furrows in his brow and the harsh lines on his face.

'Dodi grew up with the minimum of adult supervision,' he began in a low voice. 'She took her model of womanhood from the only woman she knew well. Then ... then she had an experience which led to a breakdown. I brought her here to help her forget, or at least to come to terms with what happened. I've found it so hard,' he whispered. 'For years, my work has come first and women have taken second place. They've had to fit into my schedule, I'm afraid,' he said apologetically. 'Now I have to fit into Dodi's schedule, to her whims and fancies. I'm worried that I'm not doing the right thing, that what I'm giving her isn't enough.'

'Oh, it is,' broke in Eve stoutly, trying to put aside his callous behaviour to women. He must have been having affairs during his marriage. A man like him would draw women like a magnet; they probably threw themselves at him and he was weak enough to succumb to the passions they aroused. But what had happened to his wife? If Dodi had been put into care, her mother must be dead. No wonder he looked as though he had suffered. He had obviously loved his wife very much, despite his affairs. Eve's guilt in misjudging him made her want to offer support. 'Look, it's obvious that your daughter is unsure of herself. She needs love, lots of it, and you're offering that, aren't you?'

'Yes. Is that enough?'

'It's enough for a start. After a while you'll find it easier to understand her needs.'

'I'm so grateful to you for listening. We haven't told anyone about Dodi's situation, as you may have gathered, and I certainly haven't confided my own fears before. It's a weight off my mind just to share my thoughts with someone.'

'It usually is,' said Eve gently. An irrational longing to clasp him to her heart, as she had done with Dodi, flowed in yearning waves through her body.

Seeing the expression of tenderness on her face, Matt stiffened.

'Don't look at me like that,' he said bleakly.

'I can't help it,' she whispered. 'I feel so sorry.'

'Sorry! More than that, I think,' he said softly, reaching out to take both her hands in his.

At the warmth in his eyes, Eve's heart fluttered, making her chest rise and fall quickly. She couldn't tear her eyes away from him, he was so compelling.

With a stifled groan, he pulled her to him, his arms sliding around her back. 'Please. I need someone to hold me,' he whispered in a cracked voice.

Her senses and sensibilities struggled as he enfolded her and drew her head to rest against his chest. Matt was holding her so tightly she could feel the rapid thundering of his heart on one side of her body and the echoing drum of her own on the other. His lips accidentally brushed her hair.

'Would you keep an eye on her sometimes? Perhaps even spend a few hours with her? Please, it would mean so much. You saw how she took to you. I'm sure it would do her the world of good to be with someone like you.'

'Of course,' she soothed. 'I'll do what I can.'

'Thank you.' His hands moved over her back. 'That

feels good, Eve. Oh so good! Hold me tightly, I need this so much.'

Every inch of his body was tensed, like an unyielding wall of bone and muscle. Against her temple, she could feel the tight clenching of his jaw and the quick shallow breathing which betrayed how marginally he clung to control.

'It's all right,' she whispered against his shoulder. 'Give it time. Take it slowly.' His care of Dodi had obviously taken a great deal out of him, she thought. He needed comfort as much as his daughter!

With a groan, he buried his head in her hair which seemed to be cascading in mermaid waves over her shoulders. 'That's what I need. Time. Long hours of peace and quiet to purge away all the past.' His face nuzzled gently, his warm lips trailing a glow through to her scalp. 'Your hair smells fragrant, Eve. So soft. All woman. Hold me in your arms, give me refuge.'

For a while, she murmured comforting, meaningless words to the distraught man and was relieved when he stopped talking nonsense and began to relax, his face disconcertingly nuzzling into her hair still. Sounds from outside drifted over them and they sat in perfect stillness, Eve allowing Matt to draw on her serenity. Her compassionate heart, as always, was overriding any thought of impropriety. It was not at all unknown for her to comfort people physically. Their distress and her lack of sensuality meant that it never led to anything indiscreet.

His hands absently stroked her back and he pulled her closer. And for Eve, as he did so, the embrace was changing its meaning. No longer was she feeling motherly; those small tearing sensations had begun to ski through her nerves again and she found breathing difficult.

Damn him for thinking I'm his pacifier, she thought, and realised that for the first time in her life she felt bitter. So shocked was she that she didn't notice for a moment that Matt was now pressing his warm lips to her temple, arousing an equally new tingling sensation on the surface of her skin.

'Oh!' Her lips parted in a gasp of surprise and pleasure. He stared at her, tangling his fingers in her hair, imprisoning her, then lowering his head in slow deliberation. Unable to stop him, she found her lips blooming as he began to kiss her hungrily, devouring her mouth as though there was no tomorrow.

Briefly he leaned back to search her face and she was floundering again in the satanic depths of his eyes, losing her balance so surely that she must be floating in a dream. Yet the pressure of his body was real. She was acutely aware of each pulsing inch, shouting his masculinity.

'I could crush you. Break your bones from hunger,' he growled thickly.

'No! Matt, what . . .'

'You have the most extraordinary effect on me. I want to touch you like this . . .' his fingers tentatively skimmed the bones of her face with utter gentleness, 'and savage you, like this.' That demanding, relentless mouth swooped again, its impact taking her breath away. There was such a violent power inside him, threatening to be unleashed, that she was frightened by its intensity.

'I find all this unnerving too, Eve,' he said thickly, reading her expression. 'My own reactions are a source of wonder to me. And you are a source of wonder.' He took her face between his hands and gave her a look of such raw hunger that she shook uncontrollably. 'Yes,' he whispered, feathering caresses along the line of her pouting mouth. 'We have a shattering effect on each other, don't we?'

'No, you've got it all wrong,' she moaned.

It turned into an involuntary groan in her throat, as her response began to get out of hand. The contact, and its implications, terrified her. Not on his behalf; all he wanted was a mother-figure. It was her own trembling that was so alarming. She was really enjoying the sensation of being held by this man. Be motherly, she told herself!

The groan, however, had triggered off his urgent response. 'Let me taste you,' he urged, his tongue searching the arching curves of her mouth. 'Let me show you how it will all begin.'

'What is beginning?' she muttered, trying to avoid his assault.

'Us,' he growled. With excruciatingly slow, leisurely movements, his thumbs mapped out the shape of her cheekbones and his mouth invaded their hollows.

'Ohhh . . .'

Matt muttered a sharp expletive and hauled her hard against his body, his hands bruising her spine as he moulded her curves into his unyielding, burning walls of muscle. 'Don't say anything. Don't respond. Don't do anything. I can't handle this. You're driving me out of my mind!'

He shifted his body in an intentional movement, and in alarm, Eve arched backwards, her eyes luminous in fear. This situation had gone too far! Her good intentions had been misused. All she wanted . . .

'*No!*'

'You're breathtaking,' he whispered into her ear. 'I think I'm delirious.'

'Please . . .'

'Oh yes, I'll please. Like I've never pleased before. I know it.' He reached out and touched her trembling mouth with his index finger, tracing its rosy swelling, then slid it up the hollow of her cheek to her ear. Bending his head, he nipped at the lobe which he held captive and a sharp sensation coiled angrily in the pit of her stomach.

'You are so responsive,' he murmured.

'No, I'm not,' she began desperately.

But his mouth had swooped again, his tongue stroking her lower lip, and all she could think of was the pleasure that threaded down the whole length of her body. She shuddered and his grip tightened painfully on her shoulders. As their eyes met, she saw starvation there.

'No,' she breathed, wrenching her aching mouth from his. 'Matt, you're in a state! You don't know what you're doing! Listen, I wanted to help, but not like this. I hate it, I——'

'Hush. Feel what is happening to you. Your glorious beautiful warm body.' The words were muttered into her mouth, sending shivers of excitement through Eve's breasts. 'Listen to your instincts in that peaceful, still soul. I need you, Eve. God, how I need you!'

'Stop!' moaned Eve, knowing why he was saying all this. 'It's cruel! You need some form of release at the moment, I know, but you've gone too far and you can't . . .'

'I can and I will,' he growled. 'You've made this happen, do you know that? With your gentle face and receptive heart. I never expected this tonight. I knew we would reach for each other some time, but I'd planned a slow campaign, never thinking we'd be thrown together like this.'

'Stop it! I know what you were after!' A little bit of comfort, she thought bitterly.

'Do you, indeed?' he muttered.

'Matt. Just get it quite clear that I'm disgusted with myself for letting you touch me.'

'Don't react like this. I don't want you to leave.'

'No, I'm sure you don't,' she said bitterly. 'But you can forget using me as a solver of your problems because I've had it up to *here*. I'm sick of being everyone's doormat and providing endless cups of coffee and ego-building words. I just wish people would remember I might have feelings, oh yes, even plain girls are human. We may always be in the background, we may never be considered part of the essential mainstream of life, but whenever you high-fliers come a cropper it's always us you turn to for solace. And I'm heartily *sick* of it!'

She was almost crying in frustration and anger. Her eyes drilled steel-grey knives into him and her normally soft face had turned to stone.

'Eve!'

She ran. God in heaven, her holiday was ruined! How could she ever face him again after letting him get away with such intimacies? The bay was too small for them not to keep bumping into one another. Trembling, she flung herself into her room and slammed the door, leaning against it, relieved to be safe. All these emotions within her were frightening; she hated herself, hated the kind of person he was finding inside that homely modest woman she had believed herself to be.

Now she could understand more clearly why people

acted dishonourably; there was some kind of madness that gripped you, swept you along, led you into corruption.

How tempting pleasure was. Once she had felt an austere superiority, because she was able to deny herself the delights of the flesh and others obviously couldn't. Now she was more painfully aware that her denial had more to do with a previous lack of response than any noble morality. It was no honour to be a virgin if you'd never been tempted! And the first time she had been prey to the devil, she'd succumbed like an idiot.

Matt had set her alight, creating devastation like a forest fire. Her brain seemed to have melted.

Nerves in her body defied her, leaping into life as she conjured up an image of his strong body, driving hard against hers, the living, breathing heat that surged between them threatening and promising such sweet unknown delights that she shivered alone in the empty room, half wishing that she had been born with less powerful beliefs in right and wrong.

Her body cried out for him. Like him, she was hungry, desperately hungry. But his was only an emptiness born of worry and unhappiness at the loss of his wife. She had heard of people reaching out for physical gratification as a release from mental anguish. What he had done, of course, she reasoned, going over and over everything they had said—and done—was to cry out for comfort and she happened to be around. The sensual magnetism she'd felt had only been operating one way. But what she couldn't excuse was his selfishness. He had needed someone to hold and it didn't matter what happened to the person he chose—that the sheer power of his masculinity might create untold havoc.

Eve sighed, crushing the hollowing pangs in her body. You fool, she told herself; accept it for what it was! But deep inside, she now felt a wistful longing for what might have been, if she hadn't been so ordinary and he hadn't been able to have his pick of women. His experienced touch had aroused more sensuality in her than she'd ever dreamed she possessed. If only such desires could have remained dormant! But his fervent eyes and fascinating mouth had seduced her senses and she would never return to the calm, under-sexed woman she had once been. That was what came of tangling with the devil!

CHAPTER FOUR

THERE was a hornets' nest in her head, and then her subconscious registered just one massive wasp, whirring angrily at her. She rolled over in heavy sleep, only to discover that her telephone was ringing.

'Uh?' she grunted into the receiver, wrestling with a tangled sheet.

'You know the trip to Valldemossa has left without you?' came Matt's golden voice.

'What?'

She flung down the phone on the bed and ran to the balcony, throwing open the curtains and discovering bright sun outside. A coach was just leaving the square.

'Oh darn!'

How could the morning have crept up on her like that!

Matt chattered away but she ignored him, fuming that she had overslept. Then, irritated by his voice, she slammed the receiver down on its cradle and dropped back on to the bed in fury.

Why hadn't Reception rung her? They should have checked her room. It was too much, missing the trip. She went every year. It was lovely, her favourite. And it was entirely that wretched man's fault!

She lay, staring at the ceiling, her mind relentlessly taking her back over Matt's kisses the night before, till she rolled over and buried her head in the pillow to hide her own blushes. Someone knocked on the door. The maids had come to clean and she wasn't even dressed!

'Oh come in, it's not locked,' she cried, sliding her legs

to the floor and searching blearily for her mules.

'I don't think you should stand in front of the light,' said an admiring voice.

Eve swung round, horrified.

'Get out!' she yelled at Matt.

'You invited me,' he explained, leaning comfortably against the wardrobe.

'I thought it was room-service,' she said grimly.

'It could be,' he suggested. 'Oh, it could well be.'

Eve's mouth fell open at his effrontery. 'You may think you're God's gift to women, but not as far as I'm concerned,' she said, forgetting she was silhouetted against the window.

He merely smiled and ran interested eyes over her body. 'Tell your body that,' he mocked.

A quick glance told her that he could not only see every curve outlined, but that the flimsy nightdress had arranged itself revealingly over her burgeoning breasts and their darkening ruby peaks.

'*Ohhh!*' She grabbed a beach-robe and slid into it. 'Out!' she said in a cracking voice.

'What I can't understand,' he said in conversational tone, 'is how a meek and mild girl can suddenly exhibit such fury.'

Neither can I, thought Eve. I never knew I had it in me.

'If you don't leave my room, I shall call the manager and have you thrown out and I hope the tiles break your thick head!' she grated.

'Please,' he defended, suddenly serious. 'I'm sorry. I got distracted by your appearance. I came to apologise for last night and explain about Valldemossa.'

'What has my trip to do with you?' she asked suspiciously.

'Last night, Eve. Let me explain that first.'

'Don't bother,' she spat. 'I just don't believe anyone can be so thick-skinned. Don't you understand that I don't want you in here? That I don't want to talk to you or see you or hear your voice or have anything to do with you?'

As she was speaking, her voice began to tail away, silenced by the terrible anguish in his eyes.

'Not you, Eve, not you of all people. I need you to think well of me,' he said quietly. 'I won't touch you, on my honour.'

'What honour?' she scathed. 'I've never met a man with less.'

His lower lip was caught between his white teeth. 'Please. Just hear me out. For God's sake, won't you listen first? Even murderers have a chance to speak before they're condemned!'

'You condemned yourself with your own words and actions, I think,' she said stiffly.

'Damn. Please try to understand. I've been very wound up over these last few weeks, worrying about Dodi. She's drained me of all my reserves of strength. I had no idea it would be so difficult. A few moments of your time, Eve, that's all I'm asking. Then you can tell me to leave and I'll go.'

'You do have a silvery tongue, don't you,' she derided.

'Yes,' he admitted meekly.

'Five minutes. I'm timing you from now.' It was in Eve's nature to give everyone a fair hearing. Though how he could explain . . .

He ran a hand over his face and left a haggard expression there. Eve sat down with a sigh. Agony aunty again.

'I didn't know how much on edge I was. It's been an

indescribable effort, trying to cope and appear normal. I feel I need to watch her almost constantly; she's so near to . . . well, I have to make sure that no one disturbs her and triggers off another breakdown. Sometimes I think it would have been easier if I'd let her rot in that Home. Then I see what an open and sunny girl she is, and I *know* I have to persevere. But I'm afraid it plays havoc with my own emotional and physical reserves. Most of the time I cope. Last night, I was at a rather low ebb, I'm afraid,' he explained.

'Yes, I think I do understand,' said Eve quietly.

'I hoped you would. I don't normally lean on people, Eve; they usually rely on me. I'm not used to weakness; it was very disconcerting. All I ask is that you make allowances for the strain I'm under. I've had to be that girl's rock; immovable, all-wise. I'm so worried that she'll turn out like . . . well. Last night, your sympathy— your empathy—shook me through and through. No one had seen inside me before. You saw that I was starving for warmth. No one else has even considered me. Dodi has had all the sympathy, all the care. You can get tired of giving sometimes, Eve!'

'I know, I know,' she murmured with feeling.

'Of course. You too have experienced this. Well, last night, there was such a world of tenderness in your eyes that it broke me up, I've been able to handle hatred, jealousy, anger, love and desire, but never did I expect to collapse under a gentle glance of compassion. Your tenderness soothed my wounds. It wasn't an unpleasant experience, was it? We didn't harm anyone.'

It harmed me, thought Eve grimly. 'Dodi,' she said quietly. 'It could harm her. You said she was wary of any women you spoke to.'

He frowned. 'This is a little different,' he said enigmatically.

She gave an inward sigh. It was different because there was hardly any danger of Matt developing a serious relationship with her, she supposed. She was safe to talk to, darn it!

'Please forgive me, Eve, for what happened. The last thing in the world I want is for you to hate me, or feel angry. I'd had enough. I was distraught.'

He did seem sincere. Could it be that he was genuinely so keyed up that he had become desperate for help? She walked over to the window, clutching the robe and chewing her inner lip. For a long time she tried to think rationally about what he said. He had wanted a shoulder to cry on and she'd let things go further. In a way, it was her fault; she'd misread his cry for mothering. For him, the kissing had been really a natural development and he couldn't be blamed for accepting her capitulation. Now guilt had superseded humiliation!

'Yes.' She nodded her head in understanding. He had been on edge all day, watching Dodi like a hawk. 'I accept what you say.' He'd clung to her like a drowning man clutches a straw, almost out of his mind. After all, he was too attractive and experienced to have made a pass at her under normal circumstances!

'Thank God!' he said with surprising fervour. As he leaned his head back and shut his eyes with a sigh, Eve could see he was still tightly strung.

'I think I ought to dress now,' she reminded him gently.

'Right. I'll meet you in the dining-room for breakfast.'

'Oh, no.' That might be awkward. She wasn't sure she wanted the others to investigate their 'friendship'. 'Your daughter will be expecting you.'

'She doesn't get up till late.' He was nearly out of the door.

'That's no reason. Wait! You forgot to tell me about Valldemossa!'

'At breakfast,' he smiled, and left cheerfully.

Irritated, Eve slipped into a pair of powder-blue cotton trousers and a simple white T-shirt. She hurriedly washed her face and scrubbed her teeth, then dragged a brush through her hair which seemed to have fluffed up with the constant showers she took after swimming and sunbathing. In her hurry, she snapped her last remaining twist-tie and had to abandon the idea of scraping her hair into its customary bun. Instead, she brushed it back hard away from her face.

Her hand stopped in mid-air, still holding the brush. It didn't look like her in the mirror. Instead, there was some rosy-flushed girl with charcoal eyes framed by spiky brown lashes whose lips looked as though they had been kissed all night. Her hair sprang in unruly rippling waves, bleached disgracefully by the sun.

No wonder Matt had tried it on with her last night. He could hardly be blamed if she had looked at him like that! Nervously, she walked to the dining-room and helped herself to orange juice, cereal and coffee, adding a peach to her tray. Matt was sitting at the large table she shared with her friends and he stood up as she arrived, surprising the boys into standing, too.

She kept her eyes lowered, but knew the others were agog with excitement at their unexpected visitor.

'Is that all you're eating?' enquired Matt.

Eve looked at his plate, stacked with bread-crumbed prawns, hot gammon and goujons of plaice, and scanned the other plates on the table, also groaning with delicacies from the buffet.

'I have to fight the flab,' she murmured, trying to make herself as unattractive as possible.

'I've told you before, mermaid, you are the perfect woman, the essence of femininity,' he said with obvious sincerity, making her choke on a mouthful of cereal. He smiled sweetly.

Jan's leg kicked hers but when she turned her head, Jan was innocently spooning up huge chunks of melon.

'Valldemossa,' said Eve significantly.

'Eve! Isn't the trip today?' cried Jan.

'Lord yes. Thought you were catching the coach,' said Gavin.

'So did I,' she answered drily.

'Ah, yes. That was my fault, I'm afraid,' said Matt blandly. 'You see I was just passing Reception as they were checking off the names. You were missing. I heard your name. It rang a bell,' he said innocently looking at her with his sherry eyes.

Eve glowered and sipped her coffee.

'Well, they were going to call you, but that seemed all wrong. So I said you'd cancelled.'

'You said what?' The nerve of the man!

He smiled happily. 'You must have been there before, it's the sort of trip everyone does the first time they come here, isn't it? I reckoned that if you were still sleeping, then you must be very tired. You obviously needed the rest. Had a disturbed night, did you?' he asked softly.

She shot him a suspicious glance but he seemed very straight-faced. If he only knew. Her night had been devoted almost exclusively to him and the trouble he had caused, but she was damned if she was going to give him the satisfaction of knowing that! Not trusting herself to speak, she reached over to the plate beside her, took a roll and buttered it with ferocity.

'That's mine,' said Peter mildly.

'What? Oh. Oh! Sorry, I . . .' She tried to put it back but he laughed. 'You are in a doze this morning, Eve. Let me sort this out. To be quite frank, er . . . Matt, I think you've acted very high-handedly.'

'Yes, you damn well have,' joined in Gavin belligerently.

Matt watched their defence of Eve with interest. Her mind was a raging inferno again. Why didn't he leave her alone and in peace!

'So now you've mucked up Eve's plans, what are you going to do to compensate?' asked Jan sweetly.

'Prostrate myself humbly and say that my car is at your disposal,' murmured Matt softly to Eve.

'I'm not borrowing your car. I hate driving on foreign roads. They all go far too fast. Drivers are all mad,' said Eve crossly. He'd ruined her day.

'*Have* you been to Valldemossa before?' he persisted.

'Yes, twice, but it's a trip I like to repeat,' she complained.

'What a creature of habit you are,' he teased.

'Leave her alone!' growled Gavin.

'Eve's like that,' said Peter. 'She likes things to be ordinary and repetitive and settled.'

Eve groaned at the picture he presented of her.

'Does she?' Matt's eyes scanned her face and found, to his delight, defiance there. 'Then I'm very sorry to have created upheaval in your life.' His eyes gleamed wickedly. 'Actually, my daughter and I were going there today. It seemed a heaven-sent opportunity to take you up on your kind offer.'

'Did you say daughter?' queried Gavin, leaning forwards, his fork poised in mid-air.

'Dodi, the young girl we saw dancing with Matt the

other night,' explained Eve hurriedly.

'Oh, *that* daughter,' murmured Gavin, evidently not believing a word.

'What kind offer?' asked Jan, her eyes darting from one to the other.

'Eve made friends with Dodi and agreed to come on a couple of trips with us,' said Matt casually.

'*Did* you?' Jan's surprise that Eve should have anything to do with this reprobate was very evident.

'I may have said something like that,' said Eve awkwardly.

'So, since you're sad at missing the trip . . .' Matt spread his hands in a helpless gesture.

'I—I don't know . . .' She really wasn't sure about this idea at all.

'Oh Eve, you know how you love that drive,' murmured Jan, giving her a kick.

'I don't think she ought to go,' said Gavin.

'Why not?' asked Jan.

Gavin glared at her. 'We don't even know who this chap is. He could be anybody.'

'My name is Matthew Cavell.'

'That doesn't tell us much,' said Gavin tightly.

Matt raised an eyebrow. 'What do you want me to do? Produce references?'

'You're being very rude,' Eve muttered to Gavin.

'So's he. We're not letting anyone muck around with you,' he answered.

'I have no intention of—er—mucking around. That's not my style,' said Matt gravely.

Eve wasn't sure, but there might have been the ghost of a twinkle in his eye and he seemed to be having trouble controlling the corners of his mouth.

'Well, tell us more about yourself,' said Peter baldly.

'Peter!'

Matt's mouth twisted in amusement. 'It's all right, Eve. You should be touched that these young men are so concerned for your safety. I work for UNDRO in Geneva.'

'Geneva!' breathed Jan. 'Fascinating!'

'You a lingerie salesman or something?' asked Gavin sourly.

Matt was smiling. 'It's a part of the UN that specialises in disaster relief,' he explained.

'Well! You must be all right. That's a very respectable job,' said Jan. 'Are you a pen-pusher or a red-tape man or a diplomat, or do you hand out shovels and JCBs?'

He turned his flecked lion's eyes on her and she melted visibly. 'All of those. Basically, I'm an assessor.'

'You mean you assess damage?' asked Gavin, reluctantly interested.

'In a way. Whenever there's a world disaster, a team of specialists flies out and makes an initial calculation of the most immediate needs.'

'What's your specialism?' asked Gavin.

'Man-management. I lead the team. We organise makeshift facilities from local resources till our supplies arrive. That's the most interesting part. All string, tin cans, palm leaves and chewing-gum to make emergency water containers, that kind of thing. Then we follow up with advice to the UN on what the area needs to allow them to build their lives again.'

Eve was oddly delighted. Not only did he have a legitimate job, instead of wasting his life in jet-setting around the world, but it was a worthwhile one. He must have very special qualities to do that kind of work, she thought. It was probably quite stressful; that would account for his erratic behaviour.

'I'm impressed. Aren't you impressed, Eve?' asked Jan, nudging her.

'It all sounds quite interesting,' she said calmly.

'That's the understatement of the year,' grinned Jan. 'I suppose, Matt, you travel all over the world?'

'Constantly. No,' he said, noticing her look of envy, 'it's not in the least bit glamorous. Half my life is spent in ghastly airports, waiting for clearance—we always fly off with virtually no warning—or I might be bumping over impassable roads on an arthritic camel, or trying to get local factions to work together instead of cutting each other's throats. Then there's the hours of report-writing by the light of a candle under a communal hut with fifty interested Bolivians, or whatever, breathing garlic over my shoulder.'

'You bunk down with the people?' asked Gavin in surprise.

'Usually. It's best,' he answered. 'You can see what aid is reaching them, then. Often the supplies start out from the airport but get mysteriously diverted.'

'What do you do when that happens?' Eve had become quite drawn into his background by now.

He shrugged. 'Shout, thump tables, threaten. Stride around waving rifles, that sort of thing,' he said casually.

'Gee. Ever shot anyone?' asked Peter.

Matt frowned. 'The local police tend to deal with looters. When the police loot, well, that's a different thing.'

'You didn't answer my question,' prodded Peter.

'No.'

And it was obvious that he didn't intend to. A respectful silence fell. Eve had to break it.

'How can you avoid feeling like a kind of Lord Bountiful?' asked Eve, in awe of this man's scope.

'Easy. When you're aware of the hopelessness of the situation, you feel more like Lord Useless,' said Matt grimly, his face hardening. 'When you arrive, everyone thinks that manna will fall from the sky, to say nothing of instant repairs to fractured water-pipes, damaged bridges, and a sudden inrush of twentieth-century goodies.'

'You're very committed to your work, aren't you?' commented Eve slowly, a little disorientated at the change in Matt's face. He had lost that sophisticated, rather casual expression and now seemed to be burdened with the troubles of the world.

'It's my whole life,' he said quietly. 'Or was, till Dodi took over.' He smiled. 'Even then, she'll have to take a back seat soon when I return to work. I want to get her into some kind of further education.'

'I suppose you never know when or where you're going next,' said Gavin.

'That's the trouble. In a way, I enjoy the challenge, but it plays hell with any normal social life,' grinned Matt ruefully. 'Still, I wouldn't want to do anything else. There's a great feeling of satisfaction in *doing* something, rather than just feeling sympathy when these disasters occur.'

'I've always had the urge to fly out and get stuck in when I see things like that on the television,' said Eve earnestly.

'Have you?' Matt stared at her. 'There's nothing to stop you.'

'I couldn't leave my students! They rely on me—and I'd be breaking my contract—letting the college down. Oh, I know you think that's the same kind of excuse everyone makes but . . .'

'No, I mean change your job. We could do with people like you.'

'You know nothing about me,' said Eve breathlessly. 'Qualifications, for instance.'

'I would say you have the qualifications. Think about it, Eve. I believe you could be an asset to a team. Anyway, enough of the UN. Where does that leave me and my invitation? Have I passed the entrance exam?' he said more lightly. 'Oh, and by the way,' he added in a sudden inspiration, 'it would be very pleasant if you all came up to the villa for coffee after dinner tonight.'

'Fantastic, we'd love to,' said Jan quickly, before the others could refuse. 'Then you and Eve can tell us all about your day out together.'

'Jan! I'm not sure . . .'

Matt leaned forwards. 'Why not? If you know something about the place, it would be marvellous to have you along. Dodi's feeling rather depressed at the moment. You saw that last night. She needs a friend; it would lift her enormously, something like that. Can't you help the child?'

As his face registered something more than disappointment again, she felt a pang of sympathy. It wouldn't be an unpleasant thing to do, and she would like to help.

'Dodi would like to see you again, she said so,' said Matt seriously, fixing her with his anxious eyes. 'I saw how you handled her. She's never shown affection to anyone else but me before. Have you any idea what a breakthrough that is?'

'You're very worried about her, aren't you?' Eve said.

'Of course he's worried,' said Gavin sharply. 'I'd be worried.'

'Please. Spend the day with us. It'll be fun,' pursued Matt.

'Go on,' urged Jan. 'You've never left a lame duck in the lurch before.'

'I'd hardly see Dodi as a lame duck,' muttered Peter.

'That's where you're wrong,' answered Eve. 'She needs . . .'

'Yes, Eve. She needs someone like you around her.' Matt pleaded, a message of sheer naked anxiety in his eyes.

Eve's lips compressed. She was torn, never having refused anyone help before, as Jan had said. Matt needed support. He just wasn't managing on his own. Being landed with a teenage daughter suddenly was difficult enough, let alone one who had behavioural problems, and some other unexplained reason for being on edge.

For a few moments, her thoughts see-sawed. The dice were weighted in his favour, weren't they?

'When were you thinking of leaving?' she asked quietly.

A look of pure delight spread over his face, rocking her with its purifying effect on his care-worn features, lighting up his eyes, setting them sparkling like twin suns.

'Thank you, Eve,' he said gently. 'You've made our day. I'll go over and get Dodi up. She'll be delighted.'

'Still hitting the hay, is she?' murmured Peter.

'She doesn't sleep much at night,' answered Matt quietly.

'I wonder why that is,' commented Gavin innocently.

Eve held her breath while Matt's brow creased in annoyance. 'I don't think that's any of your business, do you?'

'So what time shall we say, then?' interrupted Eve hastily.

'If I throw her under the shower, not long,' said Matt,

unaware of the interesting scene · his words were
conjuring up. 'Give it half an hour. Perhaps you could
work out where else we might go today. My cook will fix
us a picnic. See you in the car park.' He nodded to them
all and strode out, watched by everyone in the room, who
then set to gossiping about the handsome, corrupt man.

'Wow!' breathed Jan.

'You.' Eve rounded on her. 'You are very wicked! The
way you encouraged him!'

Jan giggled. 'Darling, I'm fascinated. Can't wait to see
his villa. And his cook. A *cook*! I've never known anyone
with their own cook before.'

'Hmm. And as for you two,' she said crossly to Gavin
and Peter, 'I don't know how he kept his temper.
Wondering why she didn't sleep much! She *is* his
daughter.'

'You only have his word for that,' reasoned Gavin.

'It makes sense,' argued Eve. 'He's not the kind of man
to have an affair with a teenage girl.'

'Well, you'll soon find out,' grinned Peter. 'If they get
lovey-dovey during the trip, you'll have your answer.
Can't wait to hear what happens when we see you
tonight!'

Their disbelief had worried Eve. She had believed
Matt because his story fitted in with her intuitive feelings
about him—and because she didn't really want to see
him in a bad light. A man who interested her—and
attracted her—as much as he did, must surely be
incapable of unacceptable behaviour. Yet ... would a
decent man have kissed her so expertly? Would he be so
... sensual? A warm flush suffused her skin, echoing the
crawling warmth which flowed deep within her body.

'It's what he's planning for you that I don't like, Eve.

He's a swine,' growled Gavin. 'I think he deliberately chose you.'

'What?' Eve jumped nervously at his words.

'Well, I don't know whether you realise it, but you radiate common sense and moderation. Anyone can see that this Dodi is over the top and she's giving him hell. He saw you, decided you'd be a nice calming influence and made a determined bee-line to get to know you. Cancelled your trip, hey presto, an instant unpaid nanny.'

'Gavin's right,' said Peter. 'Someone as capable as you must have seemed like a godsend. Make him pay for your time, Eve.'

Irritated, Eve lowered her lashes and stabbed her fork into a piece of peach. It didn't occur to any of them that she might be in danger of seduction! They seemed to think of her as a kind, harmless, asexual creature! And what was worse was that they were absolutely right. So much for Matt's interest in her job! He had perked up no end when he'd heard of her experience with teenagers. Drat the man!

'Maybe some of Eve's reticence will rub off on the girl. God, she made my ears ache yesterday with her chatter!' grinned Peter.

'What do you mean?' asked Eve.

'You know. You hardly ever say anything. Damn good quality in a woman,' said Gavin, ducking a pellet of bread thrown by Jan.

She considered. She seemed to have done a lot of talking to Matt. He knew more about her than she did about him. She'd never opened up to anyone like that before. But then, he'd *needed* it, hadn't he?

Half an hour later, a long sleek car drew up at the hotel, a husky horn sounding twice. Dodi's fluffy blonde head poked out of the window.

'Hey, over here!' she yelled irrepressibly, drawing prim looks of disapproval from holidaymakers.

Rather embarrassed to be associated with the couple, Eve hurried down and was surprised when Dodi scrambled out and flung herself into the back.

'Please, you sit in the front,' said Eve.

'Get in, we're blocking the road,' said Matt impatiently.

'I'm sure you'd rather Dodi sat in front,' she said.

'Oh no, he wouldn't,' laughed Dodi. 'Anyway, you can't act as our guide from the back.'

Obediently, Eve slid in and fumbled for the seat-belt. Matt's fingers closed over hers as she tried to click it into the slot and she snatched back her hand immediately.

One of his eyebrows lifted mockingly. 'You're quite safe,' he murmured.

Stupid. Of course she was safe. Weren't dull nannies always safe?

The journey was heavenly. Dodi was in good spirits and cried in delight at the scenery, drawing from Eve everything she could remember about the island. Matt drove in silence, his eyes on the road, only occasionally glancing at something if Dodi grabbed his shoulder and shrieked in his ear that he *must* look. Despite herself, Eve found the girl rather appealing, if very loud.

'Look at the trees!' she crowed. 'Just like in my fairy-tale book—all gnarly!'

'They're olives,' laughed Eve. 'And those are almonds. I think someone said there were eight million of them on the island.'

'It must be like a bridal bouquet in spring,' breathed Dodi.

'We must come here then,' murmured Matt, his eyes smiling at Eve.

'Lucky you,' she said wistfully. 'I'm in the middle of work experiences then.'

'Tell me,' said Matt.

'*Look*!' yelled Dodi as a donkey clopped slowly towards them.

'Shut up, Dodi. I was talking to Eve,' snapped Matt.

'Pig,' she said amiably.

'Work experience,' he prompted.

'I think I told you that my students have a period when they work for employers for a couple of weeks or so. Well, it's a very busy time for me—lots of problems, worries, nerves and so on. I spend my time running from one student to another, holding their hands. They do lack confidence.'

'I thought you built that up.'

'Well, yes. It's a big thing for them to trust me, and then an employer. Usually they're very anti-authority. So despite the fact that they've progressed, the experience is still nerve-racking for them. All their lives they've been told they're failures and they rely on me so much. As long as I keep telling them they're doing fine and so on, they keep going.'

'You must let go of the reins some time,' frowned Matt.

'Of course. When they've actually worked for two weeks without knifing anyone . . .'

'What?' Both Matt and Dodi were giving her their undivided attention.

'Oh, you'd be surprised,' she said ruefully. 'Their previous records are pretty violent and anti-social. That's usually the girls, of course, the lads tend to go in for fist fights.'

'Hell.' Matt fell silent and Eve realised maybe she was

worrying him. Dodi could quite easily have been one of those girls if it hadn't been for the way he and his money were keeping her out of trouble.

'Don't they have anyone to keep them in order?' asked Dodi curiously.

Eve turned around to face her. The girl looked pale. 'No, Dodi. They're not as lucky as you,' she said gently. 'Most of them have been living in squats with drug addicts and alcoholics. I had one girl who lived under the pier and a lad who slept in a cemetery.'

'Oh,' said Dodi in a very small voice.

Eve left her to think. Matt threw Eve a look of approval and patted her hand. A surge of pleasure rushed through her and she felt absurdly happy. Without realising it, she started to hum, and after a while found they were all singing together. They sped along, blissfully enjoying the freedom, the views and each other's company. Soon they were driving through the deep valley named after Mossa, the tenth-century Arab sheikh, with the mountains glaring down on them.

Matt and Dodi cried aloud in pleasure at the sudden, startling view of the hill town of Valldemossa, sheltering within fawn walls which topped a rocky crag. On its lower slopes teetered carefully tended fertile terraces, clothing the valley in green. Above the high walls reared the incomparably beautiful monastery and its ancient towers.

Hand in hand, with Dodi in the middle, they made a thorough exploration of the tiny whitewashed cells where Chopin and George Sand once lived, then stepped out into the lovely Italianate garden outside, its jade and dark green colours enlivened by wild profusions of geraniums and nasturtiums. They sat on a warm stone seat against a low wall, overlooking the almost sheer drop to the deep valley, far below. Dodi trailed a hand gently in a stone sink filled with waterlilies and golden carp. Eve leaned back against the hot wall and gazed over the beautiful, lush green valley. She wondered idly about the monks who had taken a brief rest from working in the tiny garden and sat on this very seat.

'Isn't it peaceful here?' said Dodi quietly, her small face turning up sweetly to Eve and reaching for her hand. They sat like that for some time in the sun, Matt's eyes drawn over and over again to the girl and the woman sitting beside him. In that garden, with Eve, tranquillity and innocence reigned. An inexplicable deep happiness filled Eve, flooding in lazy warmth, as Matt placed an arm around her shoulders, and she leaned into him a little. A small pulse beat irregularly at the angle of his jaw and when he turned his head to bestow a brilliant smile on her, she couldn't help but respond with a deliriously happy smile of her own.

'Enchanting,' he admired.

'Prettiest garden I've ever seen,' said Dodi in innocence.

Eve smiled at her happiness. A coach party arrived and shattered the silence, so they made their way back to the car, in a threesome, wandering through the gardens.

'It's nearly lunchtime, Eve,' said Matt. 'Any suggestions where we eat our picnic?'

There was a bay where the bougainvillaea grew, scrambling in wild profusion down precipitous slopes, backing the golden sand with deep purple. On one side, lombardy poplars hugged the skyline. Eve had gone there once with her parents on an unforgettable picnic and today she wanted to share it with Matt and Dodi. The place was so beautiful that it seeped into her heart every time she visited it. For the whole of the twenty-minute journey, she kept her fingers crossed and hoped no one had spoiled the bay, but it was just as she remembered. They had to leave the car at the top and walk through an avenue of umbrella pines, which scented the air with their resinous fragrance.

Matt reached up and rubbed leaves in the oozing resin, holding out his palms for them to sniff, then he caught each of the women by the hand and pretended they were stuck to him, so, protesting ridiculously at their imprisonment, they struggled and laughed till they all fell in a tumbling heap on the soft warm ground.

'Careful,' objected the practical Eve. 'You'll ruin the picnic.'

'Let go of my hand, you silly old thing,' grinned Dodi. 'Eve's right. Let's hurry up and get down that path. I'm starving.' With that, she grabbed the hamper and set off, skipping happily and singing about the sun having its hat on.

Matt struggled up, still holding Eve's hand. 'I haven't seen her so happy for a long time,' he said quietly. 'It's all due to you, Eve.'

'Me? Nonsense! If you'd brought her out, it would have been just the same.'

'No. I can't explain what it is, but Dodi has felt the same inner calm that I do when I'm with you. Eve, I can't tell you how much this means to me.' His thumb stroked the back of her hand, raising tiny shivers along her arm.

He was awfully close again. So close, she could hardly focus. To her dismay, Eve knew that this was one of the most special days of her life and that she was enjoying it more than she ought. She must remember her role—the reason Matt had asked her out.

'Quiet again. Such a quiet girl.' Matt's fingers traced the contours of her face.

'Don't *do* that,' she said sharply and pulled away, staring in fear with her big, wide and serious eyes.

'Sorry. Let's go and see if there's any food left, shall we?' he asked.

Dodi had set up camp in the shade of an umbrella pine which grew from the sand and had already laid out a sumptuous picnic.

'I told Mrs Turner not to do too much,' said Matt, eyeing it in disbelief.

'She loves to feed you up,' smiled Dodi.

Matt grinned. 'I do believe she's quite affectionate, under her formidable exterior. Either that, or she's expecting something from my will—all this is likely to give me a coronary.'

He was watching Dodi carefully as he said that, some element of caution in his expression, but she didn't seem to notice. 'You're far too fit for that,' she said. 'And Mrs T might be fond of you under that stiffly starched apron, but she sure doesn't go a bundle on me.'

'Well, my heart warms to her,' laughed Matt, reaching for the wine.

It must be nice, thought Eve, to cook for a man you love. She wished for a moment that she had prepared the picnic for them all.

In the shade they nibbled king prawns and fought like children over the different dips, complaining about fair shares and counting each prawn, each dunk. By the time they had worked their way through fragile pastry shells filled with chicken in coriander, and dripped luscious peach-juice all over their chins and fingers, they were in gusts of laughter.

'I don't think I've ever laughed so much,' sighed Eve, lying back, her stomach muscles quite aching from laughter.

'You should always be laughing,' said Matt. 'Your whole face lights up—you laugh with everything, from deep inside. I'm tempted to employ a gag-writer, to keep you chortling from morning to evening.'

'Please, no! I haven't the stamina for that,' grinned Eve. She squinted at the cornflower-blue sky through the branches and thought what a marvellous effect Matt had on her. She felt more relaxed with him than anyone else, was able to let herself play the fool a little, almost as if she were a child again. It had been a long time since she'd had such fun. Fun—that was it, she had never had anything as infantile and enjoyable as good clean fun. She'd always been very serious and rather ... staid. Maybe it was because of Dodi: perhaps she and Matt were unconsciously reaching out of their adult lives and into her teenage one.

Yet it hadn't been Dodi who instigated any of the tomfoolery that had arisen during the meal, it was always Matt or herself. Like children, they had squabbled and giggled, while Dodi had seemed to watch in amusement.

It *had* been fun to let her hair down. Matt was right, she must do it more often, though she couldn't see herself letting go with anyone other than him ...

Eve flushed, as the image of his strong face came to taunt her; she knew she was being drawn to him, by the way she responded whenever he looked at her—especially if their eyes met. But she would be foolish to entertain any kind of romantic ideas as far as Matt Cavell was concerned. She was on a brief holiday and their paths would never cross again. Besides, his commitment lay—quite properly—with his daughter, and then with his work. There was no room in his life for anything other than a brief flirtation. Frowning, Eve sat up, sifting sand through her fingers, as she tried to steady her mind and channel it away from thinking about Matt.

Dodi stirred, where she had flung herself to spread-eagle over the sand in the sun, a little distance away.

'I think,' she said dreamily, 'that this is the most marvellous, perfect, happiest day I have ever lived. What an angel you are, to have brought me to this heavenly island, Matt! You, Eve, you are the original Eve in the garden and this is Paradise.'

They both held their breath at the change in the girl's face. Gone was the veil that clouded her eyes, the nervous glances that showed how much reassurance she needed. Instead, her face was soft and open, glowing with happiness. Emotional tears sprang into Eve's eyes and she dashed them away, feeling Matt's warm arm around her shoulder as she did so.

'I'm going to explore for a while, is that OK?' asked Dodi.

'Take care,' warned Matt. 'It seems safe enough, but please think before you go anywhere, won't you?'

'No one's bothered about me before,' said Dodi in a small voice.

'Well, we both bother about you now,' he said, his arm tightening around Eve's shoulder.

'I'm glad,' smiled the girl.

'Please,' said Eve, when she had disappeared from sight, and lifted his fingers. 'Don't do that.'

'It's just a demonstration of affection, Eve,' he said calmly.

Not wanting to make much of it, she let his arm stay there, but trembled a little at its warmth soaking into her bones and relaxing her muscles.

'You know, it would be marvellous if you'd spend more time with us,' continued Matt, his gaze on the horizon.

'I'd like that,' admitted Eve in a low voice. 'I can see

how much Dodi has tamed down today; I'd be a fool not to notice.' She faltered, then continued, daring to voice what she longed to do. 'We could choose quite a few trips which would interest her but prevent her from getting over-excited. What do you think?'

'I think you're bewitching,' murmured Matt, turning his head to stare at her.

'I don't want to intrude, of course,' said Eve hurriedly, aware that the pulse in her throat was beating too rapidly. 'My experience tells me that she needs to be alone with you quite often.'

'And what does your experience tell you about you being alone with me?'

His mouth was too close, too curving, too damnably tempting! That smile was almost a prelude to a kiss, and that must not be. She understood how this man operated now, he was obviously easily affectionate and thought nothing of kissing a woman he was friendly with. But she felt differently: a kiss was a special commitment, and she had to be virtually in love with someone to encourage it.

'Men are an unknown factor, as far as I'm concerned,' she smiled dismissively.

'You must have learnt a good deal from your students.'

'Oh, yes, but that's different. I certainly see life with a capital L,' she laughed. 'But I don't live it, I'm on the outside. Always on the outside.'

'Maybe if you worked abroad, you'd find even greater fulfilment in more ways than one,' suggested Matt, his golden eyes warm in the sunlight.

Eve nodded. 'You've certainly put the idea firmly into my head,' she answered. 'Just as I'd settled my future in my own mind! I imagined myself with students till I retired.'

'I see you with a huge family, a baby in your arms,

toddlers tugging your skirts, and handsome black-haired sons who adore you.'

His lips were fuller now, she could swear it. The sun gleamed on the black glossiness of his hair and on the fine dark hairs that ran along his arms.

'First you alter my career, then you conjure up babies!' she laughed, a little breathlessly. 'Anyway, my children wouldn't have black hair.'

'No? I think that might depend on their father,' he murmured, then flashed his gleaming smile.

As she laughed with him, a spear like a hot poker seared through her body. Sons like him. Strong, charismatic sons to be proud of. And he would father beautiful daughters with golden eyes, daughters he'd spoil outrageously. His arm pulled her closer till their thighs were touching.

'Eve,' he muttered huskily.

She knew what he was going to do and she didn't know how—or whether—to stop him. There was so much love inside her which had to be released or she would go mad. Her long lashes fluttered and lifted in mute appeal.

CHAPTER FIVE

'OH, come *on*, you two!'

'Damn you, Dodi,' growled Matt under his breath.

'Where we going next?' she cried, running up.

'Not where I was hoping to travel,' muttered Matt, his eyes on Eve's thighs.

'The caves,' said Eve hurriedly. 'You'll like them.'

'Come on, then, the caves!' Dodi bullied the reluctant Matt into standing and dragged him back to the car.

He deliberately reached across Eve as she slid into the passenger-seat, and shut her door for her, pretending to adjust the window fastening. His warm, muscular arm, with its silken black hairs, stretched across her breasts, the movement he was making causing his arm to roll backwards and forwards across the tight fabric of her T-shirt.

'Damn thing,' pretended Matt, his face a few heart-stopping inches away. His carved mouth trembled as her breasts filled and thrust out their tips in urgent response and she quivered too, letting out her panicking breath in short gasps.

Matt's eyes squeezed shut with a pained look and he snapped back into his seat.

Shafts of slicing flame poured into the apex of Eve's body and spread through every vein. Her senses reeled at the nearness of his hips, which earlier had been almost unnoticed by her. It seemed that her nerves were alive to his every move, each subtle shift of the muscles within

90

the thin cotton trousers. And if she slanted her eyes carefully, she could see the breadth of his chest, forcing out quick gasps of heaving air and the virile strength that could hold her captive.

Sternly she chided herself. He was unattainable. He might be after a brief affair, or feminine comfort, or was merely keeping her sweet so that she accompanied them on trips. Her body and brain heard all that but took no notice. She gulped, not liking the hot sensuality that lay within her thighs. She shifted her legs uncomfortably, thinking to dissipate the sensation, but only attracted his fascinated gaze, and tiny trickles flirted their way through her nerves up to her breasts, filling them with heat and engorging them even further with singeing blood, till she felt terribly constricted in her chest and knew without looking that her nipples were hard outlines as she sat in profile.

The car swerved unexpectedly and she was thrown against Matt's shoulder. A thick curse escaped his lips.

'What *are* you doing, Matt?' asked Dodi, dragging her absorbed gaze from the scenery.

'Sorry. Attention wandered,' he said huskily.

Eve sat very upright, looking straight ahead. When she had touched his body, it was as though an electric buzzer had connected with every inch of her skin and spread its message like wildfire. She was unaccustomed to sensuality being directed at her—that was why she was unable to handle it, she told herself.

Eve fought to remain sane and sensible. But it was difficult in such close proximity to a man she wanted to turn to and shower with kisses. She knew that if she glanced at that handsome profile, she was done for: she would yearn to run her fingers down his forehead, over

his aristocratic nose, his curving lips and along his
dagger-sharp jaw. If she knew him intimately enough,
she would play with the silver-streaked strands above his
ears, maybe caress the nape of his neck, run her lips
along those scouring lines on his face . . .

Eve pulled herself together with an effort, dismayed at
her wanton, wandering thoughts. In the back, Dodi was
quiet, lulled happily by the warmth, the lunch and the
gentle movement of the car over the flat central plain
which ran through the almond-groves. Matt was silent
too and the atmosphere in the car held a strong contrast
to their earlier, more ebullient drive.

All through the journey, during the short queue at the
caves and as they wandered down into the cool limestone
caverns, Eve remained quiet and non-committal. Dodi
didn't notice, since she had cheekily pushed her way to
be close to the guide and was rapt by the spectacular
sights of the stalactites and stalagmites. Matt noticed
though, and bent his head to her in gentle concern.

'Something wrong, Eve?' he asked softly.

She turned worried eyes to him but did not reply.

'Don't be afraid of your feelings. There's nothing
sinful about them,' he said.

She smiled ruefully at his words and he seemed
satisfied that he had solved her silence and reassured her.
But she had been smiling at his innocence of her feelings.
He knew nothing of their depths. She, who for the last
few miles had been wondering what it would be like to lie
in bed with him, to feel the weight of his body . . . She
must stop fantasising and remember his motives! She
would be seriously hurt if she allowed him any liberties.

In the vast cave which served as an amphitheatre, they
sat on the wooden benches and the lights dimmed. Dodi

had been seated some distance away and had waved to show she didn't mind being separated from them.

Five hundred people sat around them yet Eve was only aware of one. She had seen all this before, but never with such intensity of awareness as she did today, and never had she felt so emotional or experienced such fervour. In a hush, the warm darkness enfolded everyone in its black cloak and Matt took advantage of anonymity by grasping her cold hand in his warm one. Like a fool, she made no protest.

In the distance, across the darkness, the lines of a boat appeared, picked out in subdued golden lights. Faintly, from far away, came the strains of soft violins, hardly perceptible, so that she tilted her head to hear them more clearly. Her hand tightened its grip in excitement. Very slowly, two boats followed the first, their lines also picked out in lights. Gently, dramatically, in a slow ballet, the boats came closer till she could see the dark outlines of the men sculling with consummate skill in total silence, over the immense lake that showed barely a ripple on its smooth black surface.

As the string orchestra played its magical concert, the two other boats slid ghostlike in an intricate and stately design, in and out of the dark arches. Five hundred people held their breath.

One of them began to stroke Eve's hand gently and moved so that his body and thigh rested warmly against her. A small tremor ran through her and he lifted her hand to his lips, kissing the palm. In the dark, her eyes flashed their distress to him, but he smiled and bent his dark head. The haunting strings were in league with him, tearing at her heart with their unbearably sweet strains, firing desire directly into her body as he slowly, inexorably grazed each finger with his teeth, exploring with his tongue and lips each ridge, each joint, each pad, then trailing with immeasurable leisure to her palm and discovering each line, finally devouring with a small moan of passion the thick fleshy pad at the base of her thumb. His teeth nipped, his mouth worked beguilingly to create an eruption of longing in her body.

This was terrible! She could hardly contain herself. It was so unfair of him, to think he ought to reward her for being kind to his daughter! How could he be so heartless—how could he treat her like this and how could her body betray her with such yearning?

'Oh, Eve,' whispered his warm breath in her ear, defying her to experience its effect and stay sane. 'I want you, I want you very much.'

She shut her eyes, willing the wild flames to stop consuming her, distressed beyond measure at her own lack of scruples. She wanted him too. More than anything.

For long minutes she sat there, forcing herself to focus on the concert, conscious of Matt's experienced seduc-tion assaulting her body, her ears, senses, reaching deep inside and vanquishing everything in its path. In any other circumstances, this would have been the man she welcomed into her heart. But she was only too well aware why he was doing this and it debased her.

The boats disappeared and she concentrated fiercely in the pitch dark, waiting for the finale of the simulated sunrise scene. Her head was forcibly turned by a strong hand; sweet demanding lips descended on hers and she quivered violently at the urging of her body. It took all her effort not to twist into him, thrusting herself into his deep chest.

Matt moved away as the house-lights suddenly blazed; watching her face, smiling a little. On the way out, Dodi caught them up and chattered nineteen to the dozen. He insisted on 'holding his girls' hands' and Eve was forced to go along with this, hating herself for wanting that contact with him and hating herself for not finding an excuse to walk alone.

It was late as they drove back. Matt seemed supremely relaxed; she was a bag of nerves and jumped at every move he made, which seemed to afford him gentle amusement.

She could hardly wait to scramble out. As they rounded the hairpin bend above the hotel, she was already beginning to gather her things together.

'See you after dinner, bring your friends for coffee,' reminded Matt firmly.

'I couldn't. I have this awful headache,' she lied. 'I think I'll have an early night.'

'I doubt that you will, I'm afraid. There's a disco on at the hotel. I'm told it's awfully loud. You'll never sleep. It'll be quieter across the bay, come over. I'll make sure Dodi doesn't do one of her ear-splitting squawks.'

'Rot you,' grinned Dodi.

Eve had forgotten the disco. For one night a fortnight, the hotel laid aside its gentle entertainments and put on a disco which drew crowds of young people from the neighbouring bay and the surrounding villas.

Seeing her hesitate, Dodi caught her arm. 'Please come to see us,' she said, pleading gently. 'I'd love you to. It's been so marvellous today, Eve, and it would be nice to have you around. Matt can bring me to the disco and I can bop around a bit, then we can all stagger back for a nightcap.'

'I'm touched that you'd want me,' said Eve warmly. She mustn't shut the child out. 'It's really nice of you, but I think I'll try to turn in.'

'Your friends would be disappointed,' Matt said wryly. 'I think they're dying to see inside the villa.'

He was right. All during dinner, the others moaned at her for letting them down, and when she heard the blaring noise of the disco, could hardly pretend that her headache would be helped if she stayed in her room. Trapped by her own lie! So reluctantly she trailed after the striding men and a lively Jan to the hotel entrance.

This time, the terrace reverberated with crashing sound. Flashing multi-coloured lights stabbed the darkness and turned the dance-floor into a rainbow nightmare.

Dodi was there already, writhing every part of her anatomy, which was clad in an outrageous white and black polka-dotted silk sheath with a long revealing slit. She wore long black ruched gloves, the diamond necklace—which threatened to injure her as it leaped around on her neck—and her blonde puff of hair had been gelled into odd spikes.

Matt sat hunched in a chair, watching gloomily as half the local Spaniards competed for her willing attention.

'Hi,' yelled Jan over the noise.

'What a racket!' complained Gavin.

'You're getting old,' screeched Jan. 'I'm going to dance. Coming?'

'Hell,' Gavin groaned.

Matt shifted his concern to Eve. 'You shouldn't be here, with your headache. Come on to the villa. The others can join us later,' he suggested.

'Oh, no, I couldn't,' she began.

'Go on, Eve, I can see some free birds,' said Peter, his eyes on some girls at the far end of the terrace.

'I'll get Dodi,' muttered Matt.

'Don't bother,' said Jan. 'She's having too good a time. We'll keep an eye on her and drag her over when we come.'

'Would you? Thanks. I can't stand this din,' said Matt.

'You oughtn't to leave her here,' said Eve hastily.

'My dear girl, if I try to extract her from those young men and prevent her from thrashing around and permanently damaging her ear drums, she'll tear me apart with her nails. Thanks, Jan. Gavin, would you see she comes to no harm?'

'OK. I'll be her daddy for the night.'

There was a slight awkward pause, though, fortunately, Matt didn't seem to notice anything offensive in the remark and merely grinned and waved farewell, catching Eve by the elbow and escorting her swiftly down the steps to the road.

Please let me keep my head. Please don't let me do anything I regret. The disco is blaring out and yet I feel nothing but the silence between us, binding us together. I'm going mad. His thigh is so hard against mine that I can feel the muscles shifting. If he doesn't move it away soon—why am I walking in unison with him? Oh darn!

'Lovely night,' she said brightly, increasing the emotional distance between them.

'Lovers' night,' he amended.

'I think the sea's gone down now,' she said conversationally, peering at the bay. 'It'll be nice and calm tomorrow.'

'That's more than I can say for me,' he replied.

'Aren't we walking a little fast?' she asked, panting as his pace increased.

'I can't get back quick enough,' he muttered.

'Yes, the disco is loud.'

'Loud enough to cover any noise,' he said. 'Any sound.'

She resisted his onward drive. 'I want to go back,' she breathed.

'No.' His voice was stern. 'Not until we've had a little time together.'

By now they had reached the gate and one arm had curved strongly around her shoulders, urging her forwards.

'I don't think that's a good idea,' she moaned.

He gave a short sigh of exasperation. 'Eve, innocence and modesty are all very laudable, but there is a limit. You don't have to keep playing Miss Untouched for ever. Damnation! I'm sorry. I can't think straight. You'll be the ruination of me.'

'Just so long as you're not the ruination of me,' she worried.

Why wasn't she protesting more? If she really tried, she could possibly wrench herself free and make a dash for it. Yet her legs were like jelly as he forced her into his lair and she was overcome with an uncontrollable shaking which merged confusingly with an equally uncontrollable excitement.

'I have no intention of hurting you. Here we are. Welcome,' he said quietly. 'Ah, Frank. Bring us the champagne now, we'll have the coffee later.'

To Eve's relief, a very English-looking manservant had appeared and grinned cheekily at her before nodding in a relaxed way and fiddling with a large bottle in an ice-bucket.

'Here, sit in the swing-chair and watch the dancers,' said Matt. 'The—er—music . . . is mercifully muted at this distance.'

Eve realised her dream, shutting her eyes for a moment and letting the swing of the sapphire lounger lull her into another world, the world of the ochre villa and its rich, vital but disturbed inhabitants. A cold glass was placed in her hands and she felt bubbles flecking her skin. She opened her eyes as Matt sat beside her and raised his glass.

'To Paradise,' he murmured, stretching out his long legs.

Silently she sipped the champagne and watched the bright lights across the bay. Up here it was cool, the patio sheltered by an arbour of grapes which hung lush and tempting above her head. Matt saw her eyes on them, reached up and picked some, leaning over her.

His fingers touched her lips with the dark purple fruit and she obligingly opened her mouth sufficiently to allow him to slip it in.

'God!' he groaned, turning away and standing with a tense back to her. 'What sort of music do you like?' he said abruptly.

'Rom . . .' She stopped in confusion, knowing her answer would be encouraging.

'Romantic?' he muttered, still looking out to sea. 'You're a very romantic girl, aren't you, Eve?' he said harshly. 'But practical, too. A good combination. I want you to consider my idea of a job with UNDRO very seriously. When I get back, I'll make sure you get some information.'

'That's very kind. Are you sure I could do such a job?'

'Oh, yes. You'd fit into the team very well.'

He was studying her carefully now and she dropped her gaze, uncertain how to respond, swinging idly on the lounger in an attempt to look relaxed and careless. 'What kind of work would I do?'

'There's always more than one woman in each team, working exclusively with the women in the area. And before you get on your feminist high horse, remember we are often in countries where men may not communicate with the women. That's where you'd come in. It sounds very chauvinistic of me to say this, but your priorities would be in organising mass cooking facilities—soup-kitchens, that kind of thing—often from anything you can find. You'd select women to run them, teach them how to ease health problems, work with the youngsters . . . oh, there's more, much more, Eve. Join us and let me train you!'

An overwhelming urge to fling caution to the winds and take him up on his offer surged through her head, filling her body with a weakness from the promise that she saw in his eyes at the closeness they would experience together. But it wasn't to be, of course. It was a lovely dream, a fantasy. She couldn't get involved with a man whose whole life lay in the shell of those eyes.

'I return to my students at the end of August,' she said in a flat, disappointed voice.

'Give in your notice. You'd be free at Christmas,' he urged.

'No! My students need me! I couldn't leave them in mid-session! What kind of person do you think I am?' she said hotly.

Matt heaved a sigh. 'Honourable. Too damn proper. Aren't you tempted?' he asked wickedly, and she wasn't sure quite what he meant.

'It's a wonderful idea, but I don't think I'm up to it,' she said firmly.

'Then think again, because I know you are,' he said sternly. 'There are few people who care *and* are strong, with the stomach to take whatever is thrown at them under appalling circumstances.'

'You're strong,' she said quietly.

He shrugged. 'It seems so. You learn to acquire a confidence, to walk in as if you know what you're doing and gently but firmly get chaos into order again. Leadership isn't an unusual quality; many people have it, few dare to exercise it, thinking they'll tread on someone's toes. Someone has to take charge. I like it to be me,' he grinned.

'You were bossy as a child,' murmured Eve.

'Insufferably. And arrogant. You wouldn't have liked me then.'

She wondered why she liked him now. Maybe it was his erratic job, where he had to commit himself deeply to a group of people and then move on to the next crisis, which made him so unconventional. Why, oh why, did he persist in flirting with her?

'I'm not sure I like you now,' she dared to say.

'Really? Come here and prove that,' he commanded.

'*No*!' she said, the word grating in her throat at the raw hunger in his eyes.

With a tightening of his jaw, he strode to her and pulled her to her feet. 'You like me,' he said, one hand stroking her bare arm, 'or you wouldn't talk so easily to me. We're the same kind of person, Eve.'

'No, that's just not true,' she said, shaking her head in denial. 'We're worlds apart. And you don't have to coax me into helping Dodi by flattering me and pretending

I'm interesting to you. It's not necessary and I find it quite hypocritical.'

Her eyes were aflame with anger at his condescension. It was like being a pet dog and fed titbits for obedience.

'It's time you took a good look at yourself,' he shot back. 'Stand in front of the mirror and compare yourself to other women you know. You have everything they have and more. Few have your depth of character, your abilities . . .'

'Oh, I was wondering when we'd come back to my job,' said Eve crossly.

'Dammit, woman, will you . . . oh hell! Here come your friends. We'll continue this later, do you understand?'

'I want you to leave me alone,' she whispered.

'Not till I have what I want,' he said menacingly.

She stared in trepidation at his angry, set face, and shivered. What was he planning? Suddenly he seemed a very dangerous animal. Perhaps this was how he looked when he had to outface looters on foreign assignments. He was intending to use her for some purpose and somehow she felt sure it was nothing to do with his daughter. Was this anything to do with the reason why he hadn't been given custody of Dodi?

Eve bit her lip, not wanting to imagine the reasons why he had been considered an unsuitable candidate to bring up a teenage girl.

'I've had a fantastic time,' cried Dodi, running to Matt and flinging her arms around him. 'Thanks for letting me stay.'

'That's OK,' he smiled. 'Glad you enjoyed yourself. Welcome,' he said to the others. 'Help yourselves to a drink and let your eardrums recover for a moment.'

'Been behaving yourself, have you, Eve?' murmured Jan.

She blushed and glared at her friend.

'I'm afraid she has,' said Matt, with a fine show of reluctance.

Gavin laughed. 'She always does. I just can't imagine Eve being depraved!'

'Really,' said Matt shortly.

'Isn't this champagne divine?' carolled Dodi. 'I've told Jan about our scrumptious day and she said we ought to take Eve on as a companion.' She pattered over to Matt and sat on his lap, winding her arms around his neck. 'Don't you think that's a good idea?'

'Eve's on holiday,' he growled as Dodi kissed his nose impudently.

'You had a lovely day, didn't you?' she asked Eve, and turned back to Matt before she could answer. 'Please, darling . . .'

'Oh, shut up, Dodi,' growled Matt irritably.

'Meanie.'

'Get off me,' he muttered. 'You're showing too much leg.'

'Don't be stuffy,' pouted the girl. 'People see much more on the beach.'

'That's different, and if you don't know it, then learn. I won't have you behaving like . . .' Matt's voice trailed off and his blazing eyes closed momentarily. 'Sorry,' he muttered.

She had jumped up and was standing in distress, twisting her hands. 'I wish you wouldn't remind me,' she breathed.

'It slipped out. I don't exactly like being reminded either,' he said in a low voice.

Dodi turned her back on him and walked over to the patio wall, and Eve could just see that she was fighting tears.

'God!' muttered Matt.

'Have you any plans for tomorrow?' Eve asked Jan hastily.

'Shopping,' she said absently, her eyes darting from Matt to his daughter with avid interest.

'No, we're not,' said Gavin. 'You've spent far too much.'

'I need some shoes,' she pouted.

'You've bought three pairs!' complained Gavin.

'It's my money!'

Eve smiled. They were always playing fighting games and they usually ended in giggles. It would distract them all till they could make their excuses and leave.

'Yeah? Money is supposed to belong to both of us. Share and share alike!'

Dodi stiffened. Matt's eyes became watchful, his body suddenly tensed.

'Then darn well share it with me,' argued Jan.

'Aha, woman,' growled Gavin, grabbing the empty champagne bottle and brandishing it over his head. 'I'll . . .'

'No, you fool!' yelled Matt and hurtled forwards to restrain Gavin.

Dodi began to shake, great moans coming from the depths of her body. Her eyes glazed in some private horror and all the time her hands fluttered as if to fend off something that threatened her. Eve sprang swiftly from her seat to hold the girl's shoulders.

Matt had pushed Gavin hard and snatched the bottle, which had smashed into smithereens against the wall as he swung it away. He was bleeding from the glass. Jan was uttering little squeals and gasps and jumping up and down on her tiny feet in panic. Peter slowly unfroze as Frank and Mrs Turner came running out, took one glance at the scene and made for Dodi.

'No, no, no!' she moaned as they tried to take her from Eve's arms. She had flung her slender body hard into Eve's and seemed to be trying to squeeze the breath out of her. Eve felt the small chest rising and falling in long hacking sobs.

'This is a madhouse!' yelled Gavin. 'I don't know what the hell is going on here, but you're all certifiable!'

'Be *quiet*, you fool!' hissed Eve.

'Whaaaat?' Gavin had been brought to a standstill by Eve's tone.

'You'd better leave,' said Matt urgently. 'Eve, Frank, help Dodi to her room.' As he spoke, he reached for the second bottle of champagne and used it to wash some of the blood from his hands, keeping a wary eye on Dodi. Small shards of glass were embedded in his palms and he winced in agony, brushing away what he could. Mrs Turner stepped forwards, but he waved her away.

'In a moment,' he muttered. 'I'm sorry this has happened. I'll pay any doctor's fees or cleaning bills. Anything. I'll be in touch. Just go!'

The stunned group left in silence and Eve heard Matt asking the cook to help him check for glass in his hands. A few moments later he appeared in Dodi's room, one of his hands lightly bandaged.

'Thanks Eve. Please stay. I need you,' he muttered. 'Some coffee is on its way. I think it's going to be a very long night.'

She was busy helping the trembling girl into bed.

'Don't go,' moaned Dodi.

'I won't,' promised Eve.

'I'm grateful.' Matt's tone was raw.

'Is there something we can get her?'

'In a way. More than anything in the world, she needs a mother.'

Eve gasped at the way he was looking at her and she knew immediately what it was that he had wanted from her. 'You mean me?'

'Who else can take on that job at the moment?' he asked impatiently.

'What happened to her real mother, Matt?' asked Eve quietly.

A look of misery flooded his face and he turned away. 'In a moment I'll tell you about it. You deserve an explanation.'

As he bent to raise his daughter and give her a mild sedative, Eve watched him with concern, resolutely crushing the pangs of jealousy which coursed through her body. It seemed that it would be a very long time before he got over his wife's death. He had wanted a mother figure to replace her and Eve was the most suitable person around. It was a daunting burden, a terrible expectation. Had they any right to demand this of her? And what was he expecting from her in the short time she had left in Mallorca? How on earth could she be of any use? It would be far worse, surely, if she made some kind of a bond with Dodi and then disappeared from her life.

Thinking hard, she managed to remove the necklace and smoothed back the mad spikes of hair. Gradually Dodi's breathing became more normal and she lay quiescent.

'Anything you want me to do, sir?' asked Frank.

'Not tonight. Leave the mess on the patio, you'll spot the slivers of glass better in the sunlight tomorrow. Get some sleep. I'll probably need you and Mrs T tomorrow.'

'Sure. 'Night, miss. Here, let me.' Frank lifted the tray of coffee from Mrs Turner's hands and laid it on a side-table.

Matt slumped down in a chair broodingly. Eve began to stroke the girl's forehead gently.

'Go to sleep, sweetheart,' she murmured. Eve's hair fell over one eye as she crooned gentle, soothing words.

Matt poured coffee for them both and came to the opposite side of the bed. His haunted eyes were fixed on Dodi's white face and Eve saw with a pang that his hands were shaking.

Dodi's eyelids fluttered then her eyes closed and she slipped into sleep.

'Poor kiddie,' said Eve, feeling very upset, tears welling in her eyes not only for father and daughter, but for herself as well.

With a murmur of compassion, Matt strode around the bed and sat beside Eve, drawing her close. Her head lay on the comforting breadth of his chest and for a while that was all her brain registered. Then came a gradual arousal of all her senses. She inhaled the fresh linen of his shirt and faint masculine aroma from his skin whenever he moved his head. She heard and felt the measured rise and fall of his chest and the pulse in his throat which she longed to surround with her lips. Her fingers, resting on the lapels of his fine cotton jacket, knew the hardness of the body beneath, and though he had not pulled her tightly to him, every inch of her was aware of the strength and firmness of him, so tantalisingly near.

Only her sense of taste had not been assailed by him,

and she had sufficient longing and imagination to know
that all she had to do to complete the sensory experience
was to lift her face and turn it slightly for their lips to
meet.

Trembling from the thought, she began to draw away
from him.

'Poor Eve!' he murmured, looking at her. 'You poor,
poor darling. What an unpleasant time I've given you. I
had no right to make you a part of all this. Forgive me for
my selfishness.'

She didn't know if she was glad or angry that she had
been involved. The tug on her emotions was unendur-
able. She made an effort to calm down.

'It would help,' she said gently, 'if you told me why
she's in this state.'

'Yes. I'm afraid that without knowing it, your friends
Jan and Gavin resurrected some unpleasant memories.'

Eve frowned. 'Joking about money?' she queried.

Matt began to stride up and down, his steps getting
quicker and quicker, his movements jerky. The look of
grief on his face planted an arrow in her breast. To see
the man she loved, like this . . .

Eve clutched at her heart, where the arrow had
pierced, and Matt swung around, spinning on his heel in
alarm.

'What is it? What's the matter?' he asked, hurrying to
her and kneeling before her.

'Nothing, nothing.' She fended him off with fluttering
hands.

'There is,' he said, kissing each hand tenderly. 'Oh,
you gentle, sweet girl. I wish to God I hadn't responded
to the soft stillness of your eyes. You seem so strong, but
you're innocent of all evil and we seem to have torn into

all your notions of humanity.'

'It's not that,' sniffed Eve. 'I just can't stand . . . people being hurt,' she said weakly, unable to say what she really wanted to tell him. It would hardly help if she loaded him with the responsibility of the fact that she was falling in love with him! She waited patiently, seeing from the conflict in his face that he was choosing what to say.

'I married Suzanne when I was a very young, very green postgraduate,' he began. 'I'd just begun to work for her father, who owned a chain of stores. He'd seen potential management-material in me. It shook him rather, when I fell for his daughter.'

'Why? He ought to have been delighted,' puzzled Eve.

Matt gave a short laugh. 'I had no breeding,' he said bitterly. 'My father was a forester—still is, for that matter. Mother worked part-time in a local newsagent.'

'Local?'

'Snowdonia, Wales. He worked for the forestry commission there. I loved it, but after university I missed the bustle of life and left home for London as soon as I could. I was dazzled by Suzanne's style of life and greedy for the opportunities it offered. My father-in-law knew that, and fought the marriage, but Suzanne wouldn't be denied her amusing, ambitious lover.'

'That doesn't sound like you at all,' said Eve quietly.

'I was very shallow when I was younger,' muttered Matt. 'It didn't take long for me to discover I'd made a mistake, that my way of life and my marriage were both alien to my real nature. I decided to try for a UN job, after watching the results of an earthquake in Iran. Suzanne wouldn't follow me to Geneva: by then, when Dodi was two, the marriage was over. My wife was bored and already taking lovers to while away the time.'

'She must have been very lonely,' mused Eve.

Matt looked up sharply, then he gave a wry grin. 'That's so like you, to be charitable. Yes, I suppose she was. I'd devoted all my energies to my career, once I'd found out that I didn't love her. She was young and beautiful; it would have been a waste not to let someone else appreciate her. Anyway, it was a mess.'

'And Dodi?'

'She came out of it badly. I hardly ever saw her—we thought it best that we didn't keep up a half-hearted contact. I never knew whether I could keep a promise to visit her or not. So she grew up not knowing me, only a succession of "uncles" and a mother who taught her how to flirt. Her model of womanhood was promiscuous sexuality and avarice.'

Shocked by the tight savagery of his voice, Eve demurred. 'Don't condemn her too much,' she said, trying to come to terms with this new image of his wife. His pain had been for a different reason, then.

'Eve, I don't care what she did in her private life, but I do object that she never hid it from Dodi. That child is very sweet and gentle underneath, but she doesn't know how to be herself. She had to stand on her own feet too early. Often she would be woken by Suzanne, having a blazing row with one of her young men. Then my wife discovered she had cancer and every one of her lovers abandoned her. Dodi watched her mother die, caring for her alone, since Suzanne had spent all her money and was in debt.'

'But her father could have helped, surely?'

'He'd died. Dodi tried to reach me, but I was in Bhutan, far from any means of communication. By the time I received her hysterical, panic-stricken letter, it was too late. Suzanne had died and Dodi had gone to the funeral alone.'

'How awful,' cried Eve, wondering how she would have coped at that age.

'When I got to the house, it was shut up. I was in a hell of a state, reeling from endless problems with the floods in Bhutan. I'd been travelling for days without sleep and could hardly think straight. Neighbours said Dodi had been taken away in an ambulance. I visited every hospital till I found the one that had cared for Dodi and they told me she was in a children's home.'

'What had happened to her?'

'The experience had been too much,' he said bitterly. 'She'd had a breakdown. Watching her mother die had been utterly traumatic. I hardly recognised Dodi: she was on strong sedatives and seemed quite lifeless.'

'I don't understand why they didn't allow her into your care.'

'You haven't seen me when I've rushed half-way around the world without shaving and without sleep.' He said wryly. 'My job is draining, Eve. Apart from physical appearances, my mental and emotional reserves are shot to pieces. I get very irate, very quickly. When I was there, a few of the teenagers had what was apparently a daily quarrel. Dodi obviously associated this with those arguments between Suzanne and her lovers, and began to go into shock. I was livid that no one did anything. I made the mistake of blowing my top; criticising the treatment and roaring my fury that she was being exposed to further distress. It didn't endear me to the authorities at all.'

'You could have had her privately nursed, you . . .' Eve hesitated. 'You had the money.'

'It wasn't money she needed pumped into her, Eve, it
was love!' he said vehemently. 'They told me I was a
stranger, that I could give her no stability, and quickly
slapped a care order on her. But I knew, from the few
short, muddled conversations that we had, that the girl
was crying out for someone of her own. I couldn't let her
down.'

'Are the police after you?' asked Eve nervously.

Matt smiled. 'No. It's a bit complicated, but my
lawyers are working on it. I'm a Swiss resident. As far as
we can make out, the only pressure they can bring to bear
is on medical grounds. They can enforce the order if I
neglect her. UNDRO have given me four months'
compassionate leave, and I made a point of staying away
from Geneva so that I didn't get drawn into any
emergencies. It's difficult to refuse assignments, when
you know of them. Anyway, I'm hoping my daughter will
be more stable after a while, provided nothing happens
to her.'

Eve stared compassionately at the sleeping girl. 'It
must have been difficult, suddenly being in charge of a
teenager. I find it hard enough even working with them
every day.'

'It was hard for her too, Eve,' he said gently. 'But
you're right, I had to show her unquestioning, unjudging
love. She's tested that a few times, I can tell you! It's been
like walking on razor-blades, trying to keep her happy
and occupied, making allowances for her and trying not
to crowd her too much. There are so many things I want
to do to change her image of womanhood, but I daren't
begin just yet.'

'From what I've seen, you've managed better than
anyone could,' said Eve gravely.

'Except you,' said Matt. 'Without you here tonight, I don't know what would have happened.'

'Without me here tonight, it probably wouldn't have happened,' she said drily. 'They were my friends who upset her, after all.'

'One day she'd have seen horseplay just like that, it had to come sooner or later,' said Matt. 'You know, I've never told anyone the reason for Dodi's breakdown, Eve, only my boss. No, don't look so flattered. My confidence isn't entirely altruistic. I want to put an idea to you. It was Dodi's suggestion, and you didn't take it seriously, but now you know my situation, maybe you'll change your mind.'

Eve sighed inwardly, knowing immediately what he was thinking. 'Not that I might consider being her companion?' she asked anxiously.

'Why not? I'd pay you, of course. I'd give a king's ransom to help her. I'd do anything, absolutely *anything*.'

He would, too, she could see that, from the intensity of his glowing eyes. He was determined to make up for all those unhappy years when his daughter had been uncared for.

'I know it would mean you weren't exactly getting a rest from everyone's troubles,' he continued. 'But you can't leave us both in the lurch, can you?' His eyes appealed to her mutely.

'It's out of the . . .'

'Eve! Dodi needs you, I need you. We had fun together today. There's no reason why the rest of your time here can't be fun, too. How much holiday have you left?'

'Just to the end of this week,' she said miserably, not wanting to leave him, ever.

'You can extend it then. I'm sure the money would

help,' he coaxed. 'Please. It would give her some stability. She trusts you. She was almost normal today. You say whatever you want to do each day, and we'll both fall in with your ideas.'

The money *would* be welcome. And if she didn't stay, would she ever forgive herself? She had been a gentling influence on Dodi, and Matt was right, the girl needed love, she needed mothering. The man ought to marry, she thought, then winced at the sharp agony that tore through her chest. He ought, she repeated firmly. In the meantime, it wouldn't hurt, would it, if she helped out? After all, she was already heavily involved in their affairs. Even if she refused, she couldn't see herself avoiding them in the Cala and she would be drawn into their lives anyway.

'All right,' she said slowly.

'Wonderful.' His breath was expelled in a great rush of air. 'I'll get your things moved over in the morning.' He looked at his watch and sighed. '*This* morning.'

'My things? What do you mean?'

'Into the spare bedroom,' he said, surprised. 'You'll have to live here, that would be part of the deal.'

CHAPTER SIX

MATT'S words were irrationally disturbing. Of course it made sense to move in. But sense wasn't foremost in her mind. She wasn't sure she could cope with Matt's vital, masculine presence. On the other hand, she wasn't sure she wanted to resist it!

Eve's brain raced while her expression remained outwardly calm. Maybe now that Matt had what he had been striving for all along—someone to mother Dodi— he would stop his half-hearted flirting. If he treated her like the paid companion that she was, and nothing else, that would be fine, however hurtful. But if he reached out for loving warmth . . .

There was no doubt that her heart was so open to him, she wanted to give him everything he asked for. She had the love to give; he didn't appear to be averse to receiving it. But it was a more limited kind of love than she had envisaged in her dreams and didn't include sharing life in a partnership. The next few moments could change her life and the way she saw herself.

'I wish you didn't think so much,' murmured Matt.

Eve's lashes fluttered in panic.

'If you're afraid of me,' he said, 'then you have nothing to worry about. I won't touch you. I'll leave you strictly alone.'

He meant it, she could see that. She had been right about his motives, then. Still she was silent. That could be just as hard to deal with!

'If you're worried about people talking . . .'

'Of course I am,' she retorted irritably, glad of that for an excuse to refuse accommodation.

'Let them go to hell,' he said. 'What's more important? Can't you see the priorities?'

'You forget, I come here year after year. I'm not having them think I'm looking after your daughter during the day and sleeping with you at night.'

His eyes lingered on her body for a moment. 'Now why should they think that?' he asked innocently.

Eve stared at him. Why indeed? Who in their right minds could possibly imagine that this seemingly contained and sophisticated man would ever want such a mundane girl as her?

'Look, I'm not luring you here to have my evil way with you,' he began. Eve flushed, embarrassed, the colour crawling up her face, taking its time. 'All I can think of at the moment is a practical, selfish arrangement. Dodi will benefit from your being here and, indirectly, so will I.'

'Of course. How sensible,' she said quietly. Inside her mind was whirling with thoughts, pain, embarrassment, longings. He had rebuked her as kindly as possible, but had made it quite clear that now his problems were sliding away and he was thinking straight, he was once more the god and she his minion. And all along, she'd known that too. Although a moth might be attracted to a flame, it was never the other way around! 'Well,' she said briskly, 'it seems Dodi is all right tonight. I'll walk back to the hotel. Then I can pack in the morning and sort out things with the management.'

'Frank will escort you back,' said Matt, relieved. 'When can you be ready—will you have breakfast with us?'

'If you like. Half-past eight tomorrow then. Perhaps

Frank can pick up my case. You realise I have to be back in England on the twenty-fourth?'

'If you say so,' he agreed.

'Well, goodnight, Matt, I'm grateful to you for explaining everything. I'll see you in the morning.'

She extended a polite hand. He might as well get used to the change in their relationship. Matt frowned, but held it briefly. 'Goodnight, Eve.'

But that wasn't, as she thought, the last time she saw him that night. Restless, after packing, with the disco now silenced in the early hours of the morning, she stood on the balcony, watching the lights of Matt's villa, flooding on to the patio. Soon she would be living there herself. It was an odd feeling. The important thing was to see herself in the strict role of companion, not as an equal to Matt. That way, she wouldn't be tempted to develop the relationship.

In her head hammered a voice: Why not? Why not? What is there to stop you?

Her gaze dropped to the dark, newly churning waters of the bay, where a trimaran was lurching wildly. Because we're ships that pass in the night, she told herself. I'm returning to my students and he'll be off around the globe. We'd never meet again. Besides, he hasn't exactly gone overboard for me. Why should he, a glamorous man like that and a nobody like me? All he ever wanted was someone to take charge of his daughter. The story of my life: help me, Eve, stem my tears, Eve, let me lean on your shoulder, Eve. Drat the man!

Her lower lip trembled. Then, as she was about to move inside, hating the beckoning pleasure of the ochre villa, she became aware of shouts from the bay. She leaned over the balcony and peered into the night. A flare rose from the trimaran. It seemed to be in trouble, and

people were already hurrying from the hotel reception
across the road to the beach. From her high position, it
seemed that the boat might be dashed on the rocks at any
minute, but in the black night, it must be almost
impossible to see where they were.

She raced to the lift and hurtled from the hotel over the
road to the beach. Matt came running across the sand,
where groups of confused people shouted and waved at
the boat. She sank back under the thatched shelter near
the beach-bar, not wanting him to see her watching.

'Who's got a car up there?' yelled Matt.

A few voices answered him, puzzled.

'Get to them fast. Shine your headlamps on the rocks.
Drive on to the beach if you must. *Move*! You, take these
torches for the moment. You that side, you the other.
Make a path with the light so the skipper can see the edge
of the rocks till the cars light up. You, go back to the hotel
and get all the rope you can find. Who's a good
swimmer? Right, stay with me. When the boat comes
in . . .'

Eve heard him describing what they were to do with
some fear. It seemed dangerous, in those breakers. But he
seemed to know what he was doing. A leader, calm,
authoritative and resourceful. This is how he must seem
to people who had suffered disasters; it must be a relief to
have such a strong, powerful man take over all your
problems. Something she'd like—not that she had
problems, really, but sometimes it would have been
easier to discuss the students with a sympathetically
strong person. To her, Matt was so different from the
other men on the beach that he shone like a beacon,
exuding power and dynamism. Pride surged in her heart
as he managed the situation with quick, easy efficiency,
his silvered temples gleaming in the light, his face urgent

and his eyes darting everywhere.

She could see the skipper now, grim-faced at the wheel in the light from the cars, his mate fixing ropes to every part of the boat that he could find. Matt was directing him to throw them out, and his fellow swimmers waded through the surf, into the path of the oncoming boat. It reared up, massive and out of control on the breakers, and Eve's heart constricted at the thought that it could easily smash one of the men to pieces. Never Matt, though; the waves wouldn't dare!

Matt directed them to grab the ropes and pull, beckoning in the others on the beach into the shallower surf, to add weight and allow the boat to suffer less of a battering on the breakers before the surge dragged her back. Under his orders, they heaved like a tug-of-war team and the trimaran had run safely on to the beach.

'*Pull!*' yelled Matt. 'Further. *Pull!*' He was taking it well out of the water, away from any likely undertow. Quickly he tied on longer ropes and ordered them to be lashed to the posts of the thatched sunshades on the beach, the waste-paper bins on the side terraces and the flagpole. Then he helped the men from the boat, catching them as they fell exhausted into his arms.

After a brief discussion, the hotel manager led the sailors into the hotel and everyone began to disperse. Eve had kept in the background, unable to help, being physically weaker than the men there, and wanting to watch Matt at work. He stood, soaked to the skin, as a few men slapped his back in congratulations, which he accepted absently, then trudged up the beach to the villa.

'Matt,' she called, then regretted it, clutching her hands to her breast.

'What are you doing up at this hour, Eve?' he asked, coming closer.

'I heard the shouting. How will they get the boat off again?'

'Oh, no problem,' he said. 'If we can get block and tackle, I could fix two points on either side of the rocks there, then use the pedalo tractor pulling in the opposite direction to ... What are you laughing at?' he asked, hurt.

'You're so unlike the men I know,' she grinned.

'How?'

'They're all rather weak and they lean on me. I don't mean Gavin and Peter, they're different, that's why I like them, but they're not . . .' Her voice stammered to a halt.

'Not what, Eve?' he asked huskily.

The wild waves which thundered through her body were far more dangerous than the breakers in the bay. There was no reason, none at all now, why they shouldn't become . . . closer.

'Matt . . .'

'Shh,' he murmured, placing a finger on her lips. 'Say nothing.'

His finger traced the line of her mouth, sending delicious shivers up her back. Then, with a muttered exclamation, he drew her to him and she felt the cold wetness of his clothes, then the warmth within.

'Can you feel my heart?' he whispered.

He drew her hand there, and she felt the mad thudding, as though he harboured a wild, untamed passion. She couldn't believe it was for her specifically; time had probably increased his hunger, since it must have been a while since he had had a spare moment to devote to a woman. Her body leapt into life, disregarding the fact that it could be any woman here, in much the same way that he could have been dancing with anyone when she first saw him; both expressed a release of physical action, held for a long time under tight control. It was all she could do, to prevent herself from arching wantonly into him.

'Eve,' he breathed. 'You arouse me like no other woman. I thought I knew it all, had savoured all, could exhibit masterly self-control. No woman has ever reached so deep and driven so much to the surface before. I feel like a raw youth again, wary of mistiming everything. I can't think straight. Even here, on this beach, soaking wet and cold.'

'Oh,' gasped Eve. 'People will . . .'

'Here.' He pulled her into the shelter of the rock, away from prying eyes. 'I want to love you till you can't think straight either.' His voice had grown darkly husky with passion. His mouth swooped, his tongue stroking her lower lip, and all she could think of was the pleasure that threaded down the whole length of her body. She shuddered and his grip tightened painfully on her shoulders. As their eyes met, she saw starvation there.

'Matt I don't think . . .'

'Good. I don't want you to think. Listen to your instincts for once, in that peaceful, still soul. I need you, Eve!'

His mouth slid over hers again and his tongue gently parted her lips, exploring erotically the soft inner moistness, startling and delighting Eve with the sensations he was creating. Every nerve she possessed was concentrating on wringing the greatest pleasure from the movement of his curling tongue as it toured the dark cavity of her mouth. For one, mad moment, her own tongue flickered to meet his and a powerful shock ran through Matt's body.

She was astonished that such a small involuntary movement could create such trembling. It was as though

all his muscles had turned to fluid for one glorious
moment. Her head swam with the potency of her power.
It was a sweet strength, to affect such a dazzling man.

His kisses deepened, his hands forced her head harder
into his lips, driving all rationality from her brain and all
she was aware of was the enveloping potential of their
bodies, aching to merge into one. She was helpless to stop
him. Every bone in her spine was being caressed with
gentle fingers, which slid languidly down, moving to her
waist, savouring its warmth. Eve untangled her hands
from his hair where they seemed to have been battling in
a frenzy of their own and placed them against his chest,
pushing gently, her long brown lashes fluttering in
panicking crescents on her cheeks.

'God, you're beautiful,' he groaned, kissing her eyes. 'I
don't know what to kiss and what to touch first.' His
mouth decided for him, and turned its attention to her
slender throat. A sigh of breath escaped from her lips as
he did so. The sensuality of his gesture, and the heart-
stopping curve of his jaw as he nibbled and tasted her
perfumed skin, made her hands fly to her breasts to
assuage their swelling need.

'Let me,' he murmured gently.

'No, Matt,' she protested, her lips thick and as bruised
as poppies from his ravaging mouth. She had to think,
she needed a moment to . . .

His breath rasped in her ear as his hands unzipped the
upper part of her dress.

'*No!*' she husked.

To her partial and contrary dismay, he muttered
something under his breath, leaned back a little and she
felt the zip burring over her skin as it was fastened again.
There was a crooked grin on his face, a grin of
disappointment and resignation.

'Another time,' he promised, his tawny eyes hazy with desire. 'Perhaps I should have a quick swim, let the water cool me down.'

'Don't! It's not safe, you . . .' She broke off, confused at his raised eyebrows, feeling foolish. It must seem to him that she cared. 'I'd have to dash in and try to save you,' she said quickly. 'I never quite managed the life-saving badge, I'm afraid. Matt . . .' Now they were standing a little apart, she was a little appalled at what had happened. How on earth would she handle the situation at the villa?

'Before you ask,' he said gently, 'please don't let this change anything. I need you to keep a friendly eye on Dodi and to give her a model of womanhood that she never had. You have my word that I won't embarrass you at any time, nor will I ever come to your bedroom. I promise this Eve.'

'Oh.' Her hands shook. 'Goodnight.'

As she walked back, alone, she struggled to calm her raging thoughts, but could make no sense of them other than the fact that the impossible had happened. Matt Cavell had kissed her with more than a passing interest and she was so deliriously happy that she wanted to skip all the way back and hug herself, over and over again. Stupid, foolish madness it might be, and she was bound to be hurt, but she didn't care!

Eve's first move, when she had a spare moment, was to write a long letter to her parents, explaining why she was not returning as planned. It was difficult to write. For the first time in her life, she wasn't being totally honest with them, or with herself, by omitting to mention her emotional entanglement.

It took only a short time before a garbled version of

Eve's employment spread through the Cala. Eve was quite amused at the altered circumstances. As far as Dodi was concerned, there was no difference, but Matt treated her with a distant politeness. And Eve knew her place.

For the next few days, she was kept happy and busy. Most of the time they went around together, though sometimes she and Dodi lounged around on the beach, when Eve made sure that the girl was drawn into the groups.

In a threesome, they went sightseeing and shopping. They lunched in a pavement café, vying to choose the ugliest fish on the crushed ice and lashing out extravagantly on punnets of huge strawberries, but mostly they enjoyed spending time at the beautiful villa and in the Cala, swimming, sunbathing and chatting. Dodi had relaxed wonderfully, and in consequence so had Matt.

True to his word, he didn't make even one pass at her. There was the occasion when Dodi went early to bed and they were alone on the terrace. He began to tear at his lower lip with his teeth, as though he found the situation of employer and employee in such companionship a little difficult to handle. When she rose to leave, there was a definite relief in his eyes. Despite living so closely with him, Matt seemed more of an exotic bird of paradise than he had been before. She became aware of her sheltered life in the vicarage. In comparison, Matt awed her with his practical experience of the world and his obvious authority. She had been very ingenuous to imagine he would be seriously interested in her; she was very dull. His world was on another plane.

Eve recognised her symptoms as being akin to hero-worship and she chided herself severely. Her heart leapt whenever he entered a room; she tensed when he came close, and she became rattled, finding it difficult to maintain a quiet poise.

One morning, she and Matt were breakfasting alone when he said abruptly, 'I'm going away for a few days.'

Something hit Eve like a cold douche of iced water. 'Oh?' she managed, feeling desolate.

'Things are OK here. Geneva needs me.'

'Geneva?'

'Don't repeat things I say,' he said irritably. 'You heard. It's an emergency. The department is over-stretched. Half the staff have gone down with 'flu. What with El Salvador, Guatemala, Uganda, oh, I could go on forever. Bolivia is the current problem. We can't get medical supplies through. Someone has to organise transportation.'

'You,' said Eve in a dull voice.

Matt jumped up and paced the terrace like a caged tiger. 'There is no one else. Each unit is doing about four other jobs at the same time. Eve, I must go! The Director said he'd quite understand if I couldn't lend a hand, but . . .' Matt's teeth chewed away and his voice lowered. 'I can't let them down. Every hour I delay could mean someone's life if we don't get things running smoothly.'

'So you'd go immediately,' Eve stated.

Matt nodded. 'You can cope, can't you?'

At her cool smile of agreement, he turned towards the crags at the end of the peninsula. 'I don't want to go, Eve,' he said quietly.

'I'm sure you don't,' she said, in a matter-of-fact tone. Then her breathing quickened. 'Is . . . is there any danger?' she said, her hand on a wildly palpitating heart.

'Danger of what?' he asked, his gaze fixed on a distant rock.

'You, being hurt.'

'That. No. You'll be here when I get back, won't you?'
he asked in a tight voice.

'That rather depends how long you'll be.'

'No more than ten days.'

'I'll be here.'

'Then I'll leave now. I'll stop in on Dodi. Frank will
hand over any money you need. 'Bye.'

I hate goodbyes, thought Eve bleakly, as she watched
him drive away an hour later. How much worse it was
going to be, at nine twenty-five in the morning on the
twenty-fourth of August!

Soon it seemed to Eve that she had always lived in the
villa. Jan, Gavin and Peter had returned to England,
after a noisy farewell at the hotel. Jan had made some
very odd remarks when Eve had tried to fix up the date
they would meet the next year. She had suggested they
might see each other before that, and Eve might be
elsewhere next summer, but had left on that enigmatic
note. Jan was probably planning some reunion in
England, and intended to persuade her to holiday
elsewhere with them.

Eve became very fond of Dodi. They had made many
friends on the beach and during the coach-trips they
took. Every day was rather like one huge house-party.
Without Matt's unnerving presence, the holiday was
turning out to be very enjoyable after all.

During their evenings together, Dodi confided her
interest in working with children. Eve promised that she
would find out about Nursery Nursing courses, and was
pleasantly surprised at the enthusiasm that her suggestion aroused. She could see that the girl would be ideally
suited for that kind of work and together they made
plans.

Occasionally, Dodi would speak of her home life. It was amazing that such an irregular and inconsistent approach hadn't made her totally uncontrollable and precocious. Suzanne had lived selfishly and promiscuously, it seemed; no wonder Matt had become disillusioned. The lack of stability had made Dodi very insecure, but she was learning that her own naturally sunny nature made her popular and that gave her enormous confidence.

Eve was also blooming. She bought some stylish clothes in Palma, loving her new image, and was quite happy never to scrape her hair back into a bun again. She felt younger and prettier than she ever had, the golden tan deepening the colour of her eyes and giving her skin a warm, healthy bloom.

Once, she rang her parents to keep in touch, and they had laughed at her fulsome descriptions of the island and the life she was leading there. That made her stop and smile. She *had* changed—and she rather liked it!

But whenever she allowed herself time to think, it was of Matt. He filled her mind, lurking there, ready to invade it whenever she was careless enough to let him slip from her subconscious into more vivid images. Suddenly she would see his body, in all its golden glory, the sun glossing the black hairs on his chest where they sprang so vigorously. Or she would be shocked by the memory of his mouth, slowly, pleasurably, descending to hers which was opening like a parched flower to a shower of rain.

It was then that she would worry about his safety.

'Matt hasn't rung. Do you think he's all right?' Eve asked Dodi one night, as they returned to the villa after coffee with friends in a local bar.

'He never rings when he's away. Usually it's too

difficult, sometimes impossible. So he concentrates on the job and forgets everything else on purpose. Even if he's near civilisation, he just gets on with work and turns up like a bad penny,' replied Dodi.

She stopped at the bottom of the steps to the villa. 'Like that,' she added, grinning.

Eve followed her gaze and found her heart thumping violently. A tall figure, unmistakably Matt from the width of his shoulders, stood on the patio, silhouetted against the golden light from the lounge. Dodi was racing up the steps and Eve followed slowly, trying to breathe calmly. Her stomach was a painful void. She wanted to run too, wanted to laugh with delight and fling her arms around him like his daughter. Instead, she fixed a pleasant smile and welcomed him coolly.

'It's nice to see you again, Matt,' she said, thrusting her hands into the pockets of her coral dress to stop him seeing that she had the shakes.

He had watched her progress over Dodi's head, a closed look on his haggard face. He looked a stranger, almost a ruffian, his clothes crumpled and dusty, the grey streaks at his temples even greyer in contrast with the black growth of beard and the scouring lines on his face deeply etched.

'Hello,' he said wearily.

Dodi leaned back to look up at him.

'You look *awful*,' she said.

'Flatterer. I'm going to bed.'

'Pig! I . . .'

'Don't push me!' he yelled. 'Leave me alone. It's been hell.'

Eve's hand reached out to touch Dodi's arm and stop her understandable reaction.

'In the morning. We'll chat over breakfast, maybe,'

she said, eyeing his bleak eyes in alarm.

But they didn't. Matt stayed in bed and only appeared at lunchtime. He was still obviously shattered and hadn't even bothered to shave or comb his hair. Eve and Dodi hung around the house, waiting to see him, and they were subdued by his apearance.

'Anything I can get you?' asked Eve quietly.

'No. Dodi, go and play. You're fidgeting. I can't stand it.'

'*Play*?! But . . .' She saw the thunder in his face and obeyed.

Eve quietly drank her coffee and kept replenishing his.

'Any more fresh orange?' he asked.

With a graceful movement, she rose and poured out a tumblerful. As she put down the jug, his hand caught her wrist gently and he laid it against his cheek.

'I could have done with you out there, Eve,' he said quietly.

She let him rub his rasping beard against the back of her hand absently.

'It was bedlam. I can't tell you what it's meant to come back to your tranquillity. It kept me going all that time. Whenever I felt I was going mad, I thought of you.'

'Oh, Matt!' she breathed, entranced by his words.

'I've never had anyone who gave me so much strength—or,' he said ruefully, 'so much weakness. My knees just go when I think of what I'm going to do to you.'

His mouth began to savage her palm and she snatched her hand away, suddenly realising her dilemma. Time was running short.

'What is it, Eve?' he asked. 'You're holding back on me. There's no need.'

'I . . . I'm flying home at the end of the week,' she blurted.

'What!'

'You *know* I am, I said . . .'

'But . . .' He shook his head, as if to clear it.

'You'll be able to pay me up to date on Friday, will you?' she asked tightly.

That made him look up. 'God! You really know how to twist the knife in a wound, don't you?' he said bitterly. 'Sure. I can pay you. Handing out money is a simple operation. You mercenary bitch!'

Eve was about to retort angrily, when she realised from his face that the experience in Bolivia was wreaking havoc with his emotions. She bit back the words and for the rest of the mind-numbing dreary week kept her distance from him.

It was on Eve's last full day that the inevitable happened.

She had woken early, her sleep deeply disturbed by some imminent emptiness. Leaving Matt was going to be the hardest thing she had ever done in her life. She'd hoped that he would offer to make contact with her some time, or remind her about a possible job with UNDRO, but he had been unbelievably irascible and unapproachable. He'd had his money's worth and that was sufficient, it seemed. She would return to her ordinary life and he to his extraordinary one.

She had no excuse to stay—her students needed her; she had her own obligations to cope with and she couldn't abandon them. She had never done anything dishonourable in her life.

For some time she sat quietly at the window, staring mindlessly out to the fathomless sea. Then, as a slight lightening of the sky heralded the dawn, she dressed and climbed to the top of the low sierra above the villa, to see the sunrise. The first pale shafts hit the rocks at Punta de la Troneta and slowly the petals of the dawn flooded the great rock with a rosy glow. A feeling of utter calm descended on her. Whatever happened, she had known for a short while a man she would never forget for the whole of her life. Despite the fact that he had caused her so much secret pain and destroyed her old image of herself, he had immeasurably enriched her life. Never again would she be merely a receptive and passive onlooker. She knew now that she was capable of passion and that she would hold it in her heart for him, for ever.

'Well,' she said brightly at breakfast. 'It's my last day. What shall we do?'

'Oh, spend it here,' said Dodi, with enthusiasm.

'Oh.' Eve was disappointed.

'Look at the sea,' said Dodi. 'It's like glass. We can't waste that today. I can't think of anywhere better to spend today, can you?'

Surprisingly, Matt tagged along with them, for the first time since before he went away. At the water's edge, he slipped off his shirt and bent to undo his shorts and as he did so, the unexpected hot sparks, darting fiercely into her loins, made her quickly avert her gaze. Clad only in brief white trunks, he patiently waited for Eve, watching with hooded eyes as she awkwardly unbuttoned her dress.

Dodi, who stripped faster than anyone she knew, had grabbed a lilo and was charging into the sapphire sea.

'Last day, Eve,' said Matt quietly.

A lump came into her throat.

'Nothing to say?' he asked.

Her chin dropped and she pretended to fumble with her costume, then pushed past him and walked blindly into the water. For a while, she swam in the shimmering blue, dazzled by the glassy reflection of the sun, and

choking on the lump that had risen in her throat, till the
sea had wrapped its silk around her in a soothing balm.
By now, she was quite a way out, but Matt had followed
her, towing the other lilo. He heaved himself on to it and
paddled up to her as she floated on her back.

Together, in the hot sun, they lay in the mirror-smooth
water. Hardly a ripple disturbed the glittering surface
and Eve's thoughts drifted gently, dreaming of being
caressed and lulled by Matt's sure touch.

'Come on the lilo,' he murmured softly.

'Mmm, all right,' she agreed lazily, waiting for him to
get off.

Yet when she pulled herself up, he reached over and, in
a precarious balancing operation, hauled himself to lie
beside her.

'No, don't move,' he whispered. 'You'll tip both of us
in.'

'But . . .'

Her protests were stopped by his mouth. Just one,
sweet, agonising short kiss and his lips moved away as he
busied himself with paddling them along, his body
virtually lying on top of hers. Eve kept still, trapped by
his weight. They seemed to be moving towards the little
cove next to the Cala, one which could only be reached
from the sea. Here, near the rocks, when she looked
down into the depths of the sea, it was like looking into a
faceted emerald.

He had slipped from the lilo. Eve raised her head and
saw he was towing her into the tiny crescent of sand. The
water lapped at her feet, the lilo was beached.

'You can't leave,' said Matt quietly.

She was stilled. He sounded so certain. 'One large 747
on the tarmac says I can,' she tried to joke.

'I don't want you to go.'

'I must,' she said lightly, not daring to acknowledge her feelings.

'Why?'

'You *know* why. I must interview for my next group and organise the courses. You know yourself how time-consuming it is to organise other people. It's the busiest term. I've got last year's group and the new entries to contend with.'

'I need you.'

'A whole college department needs me. Sorry, Matt, but that's my life, isn't it? I already have commitments.'

'How can you be so hard?'

The word shocked her. She was being practical, for heaven's sake!

'You don't want to go,' he muttered.

'Of course not, it's lovely being on holiday,' she fended.

'Damn you!'

The words were growled with such ferocity that she began to rise, only to be forced back by Matt's hands, gripping her shoulders. He straddled her, glaring.

'You've just about pushed me to the limit,' he muttered. 'Don't open your eyes at me like that! You know how much it provokes me!'

Bewildered, Eve scanned his face, and was frightened by what she saw. It was as though all the despair and frustrations of his last few years had welled up and were about to explode in a bombshell of violent, shattering emotion. Timorously, she reached up and touched his face in compassion, to ward off his anger, directed so unfairly at her.

'Eve,' he whispered. Then she felt his breath in her ear, as he whispered 'Eve' again. The rush of moist warmth and the honeyed tone of his voice stirred her body. His tongue gently curled around the intricacies of her ear and his teeth sharply nipped her lobe.

'Oh,' she moaned.

'That's it, give in. Try this.'

He buried his face in her neck and savaged her throat till the feel of his teeth and tongue drawing the flesh had rendered her delirious.

'Shall I kiss you?' he murmured against her mouth.

'No, no.'

Her lips parted in an unconscious invitation.

Matt's gaze burned into the darkening, fear-ridden grey eyes that were fixed on him like a mesmerised rabbit and compelled her to surrender. But he didn't lower his head, even when she fiercely blotted out the image of him looming above her so menacingly, so achingly desirable. She waited in an agony of blind expectation. Instead, his thumbs gently stroked her upper arms. That was all. She lay there, the sun warming her body, flames licking within from her own desire, trying to overcome the languor that stole through her bemused mind. He seemed very much in control of himself. She felt a wild urge to break that control.

Eve found her breathing had become ragged. She ran her tongue around her parched lips and her hands stole to his chest where her fingers tangled and tugged at the dark hairs that sprang there.

'Oh, please,' she moaned.

'Why don't you take what you want?' he asked softly.

Her eyes flew open to meet his, melting, golden, glowing and offering her—what? An afternoon's sensual exploration on a beach in return for . . . Was he trying to persuade her to stay? Eve's eyes shut again tightly as she tried to forget him, tried to forget the insistent rhythm of his fingers.

A shudder ran the whole length of her body. It arched

to meet his, of its own accord.

His quick intake of breath precluded a swift movement. In one easy flick of his hands, his fingers had slipped under her straps and drawn them down her arms. She could have reacted and covered herself again but she didn't want to. Lazily she looked along the length of her body, the swelling breasts and hardening, dark crushed centres, the nearness of him as he knelt above her. All he had to do was to touch, but he didn't! Her body curved up to him; she grasped his arms and drew her nails down them in desire.

'What do you want, Eve?'

'Please!'

'Tell me,' he coaxed softly. 'Tell me what you want.'

'Touch me,' she whispered huskily.

'I am.'

'Not there!'

Silence. Eve felt like an empty vessel, whose only function in life at that moment was to be filled with kisses, touches, covered by his mouth and wandering hands, and still he did nothing! How could he be so unaffected!

She raised agonised eyes to his and angrily grabbed the hair at the back of his head, pulling him off balance and tearing at his mouth with her lips, trying in her desperation to kill some of this unbearable longing.

Willingly, he took over the assault, matching her frenzy, and they rolled over and over on the beach, clinging to one another tightly and attacking each other's mouths in a climactic rage of long unfulfilled passion. She had been famished all the days of her life and was ready for that hunger to be satisfied. Ready to seduce this half-willing man, whatever his reasons were for making a pass at her.

'Say what you'd like me to do,' he said throatily.

'Ohh!' Eve threw caution to the winds. 'Touch my breasts. Hold them.'

The pleasure, as he cradled their soft weight in his long tanned fingers, was exquisite.

'And now?' he murmured, moulding them in warmth.

'Please don't ask,' she whispered.

His index finger reached out and slowly circled. A chorus of nerves focused on that spot, till his mouth descended to the other breast and sweetly suckled. Her body electrified, Eve cried out aloud in pleasure.

'Good girl,' he muttered thickly. 'Tell me more. Tell me what you like.'

'Your tongue,' she moaned, 'and your teeth. Your mouth.'

Small shooting pains urged her to claim his hands as he tugged at her breast, his bruised mouth bringing each firm rubied tip to its fullness. This time, she pushed his hands down her body. For a moment, they rested on her waist, resisting, and he paused, a long, tense postponement of pleasure.

'God!'

And he was gone. In a flurry of spray, he had run into the sea and plunged in a headlong dive, swimming back to the Cala. Eve sat up, an awful hollow feeling sucking at her stomach. What had she done to make him leave? Had she frightened him off? Was she so unappealing that he couldn't make love to her, even if it ensured Dodi's continued companionship?

Once again, she had walked willingly into her own humiliation. For nearly an hour she sat on the beach, trying to stop shaking from the urgency of her needs. Then, only slightly recovering her composure, she pushed the lilo into the water and paddled back slowly. The sun, crowds and laughter all around only mocked her.

Eve trudged despondently up to the patio, hoping to avoid anyone. But Matt and Dodi watched her arrive, laughing at some private joke. About her, probably. Defiantly, Eve flicked back her dripping hair and gave Matt a cool look, but he smiled gently and asked if she had enjoyed her morning.

'Mmm,' she answered, not trusting herself to speak.

'Well, I hope you did something you've not tried before,' said Dodi innocently. 'You always should on your last day.'

'Shut up, Dodi,' muttered Matt. 'Eat your tortilla.'

She stuck her tongue out at him and grinned at Eve. 'You look awfully flushed, Eve. Have you been exposed to the sun?'

Matt shot her a worried look. No doubt he was wondering how he was going to cope if he was called away and she wasn't around. Sickened, she pushed away her plate.

'Eve! Aren't you well?'

She gave him an icy look. 'I'm going to take a siesta. I'm not hungry. Excuse me.'

She stripped and showered for ages, cooling down a little. In the half-darkness, she padded over to the bed and slid naked under one sheet, a small involuntary moan escaping her lips as the soft cool material caressed her body like a whisper. It was the first time she had been naked anywhere other than her bathroom and she felt utterly depraved. Perhaps it would have been better if she'd dressed in woolly socks and a hairnet, she thought ruefully.

Her brain fought for sleep, her body battled to stay alive and won. Every toss and turn seemed to inflame her senses more as her skin slid under the sheets and her hands unwittingly came into contact with her flesh.

'*Oh drat*!' she spat, flinging the sheet back and throwing her arms back over her head.

'Difficulty sleeping?' murmured Matt.

She reached for the sheet, but he'd whipped it off the bed and his eyes darkened to see her body, a gentle golden brown against the undersheet, stretched to its full womanhood.

CHAPTER SEVEN

'YOU said you'd never come to my room!' Eve accused, her voice breaking in mid-sentence.

'I know. All this time I've managed to keep away; but we have something between us that needs finishing if I'm not to go mad with desire!'

Eve was powerless to move. The look in his eyes betrayed his intentions and she didn't care, she welcomed them. This would be the one and only time she behaved so recklessly, she thought, and it would be worth it. She had to satisfy that raging need within! Defeated gloriously, she lay back again, only the fact that her hands clutched at the sheet underneath showed her apprehension. One knee rose and angled over the dark brown triangle of hair in shy defence.

Matt gently ran one hand over that knee, then bent to kiss her toes, one by one, lifting her foot to his mouth so that he could still watch her reaction.

'What perfect feet you have,' he murmured, running his tongue under the high arch. 'Dainty, dancer's feet. And . . .' each toe was drawn into his soft, warm and moist mouth, while Eve fought to keep a hold on her senses '. . . such sweet-tasting toes. I wonder,' he continued idly, 'if the rest of you tastes so luscious?'

His hands ran smoothly up her calf, coming to rest against the softness of her inner thigh and at his questioning look, gold fires aflame in his tiger eyes, her hand flew to her mouth defensively, stopping the cry of 'Now!'

The hard planes of his face smoothed out and a softness replaced them.

'At last,' he said. 'I intend to realise all my dreams soon, you gorgeous creature. You've been as difficult to capture as any mermaid. Or any croaking butterfly.' He smiled gently.

'Capture?' she breathed. She had been enslaved for as long as she could remember.

'Yes, my sweet. I knew how easily I might damage your delicate scales if I rushed things. Fortunate, isn't it, that both mermaids and butterflies have scales?'

What was he talking about? wondered Eve to herself. Why didn't he . . .

'Are you inviting me into your body?' he asked huskily.

She couldn't answer. Couldn't be that brazen. But he found the answer from her unfairly, by softening her mouth with his, feasting hungrily. His fingers threaded through her hair, as his kisses deepened in passion and her own fingers fumbled blindly with the buttons of his shirt, till she sighed in her throat when she could finally press her palms against the heat of his chest and begin to explore its contours. Her mouth slithered along his jawline, to the hollow of his throat, then stealthily crossed his torso.

'Don't!' he muttered as her mouth covered his nipple. 'I'm going to make love to you,' he said, raw hunger in his voice. 'To be inside you at last. Don't touch me there, Eve, for the love of God, I shan't be able to keep control! I don't want to ruin our first lovemaking together.'

Frantically he sat up and dragged off his shirt,

watching her from narrowed eyes and judging her
compliance. Eve averted her gaze as his hands went to
the buckle of his belt, struggling a little in his haste.
There was a rustle of clothes and suddenly his warmth
had returned to her, this time as a burning, fevered
nakedness.

'Eve. My Eve,' he whispered into her mouth.

'I want you,' she moaned.

'Then you shall have me,' he promised. 'Soon, very
soon.'

His lips savoured the length of her throat and ran along
her shoulders. She felt his hands slip to her breasts and
with trembling fingers arouse them till they were hot for
his mouth. Nothing but the final act of love would satisfy
her now.

Without knowing what she did, Eve began to writhe
against him, feeling the satin of their skins sliding in an
exquisite rhythm, the rock-hard muscle of his thighs
tensing and bearing down on her.

'Wait,' he commanded, rolling back on his side. To her
dismay, his finger casually traced the lines of each rib
while she complained and begged for his touch to
descend. He laughed quietly and kissed her again,
consuming her in the smouldering embers of his eyes.
The fever raged in her brain as he tormented her, lightly
stroking the soft curves of her body. In a gesture so
blatantly erotic that she felt her heart contract, he placed
his index finger in his mouth and then ran it lightly over
one jutting nipple. Too lightly.

'Again,' she breathed.

'Again,' he answered.

'More.'

'More.'

'The other one,' she yearned.

'Mmmm.'

She waited for that last, equalising touch. It didn't come. Her drugged eyes opened slowly, heavily, and focused through a curtained cloud. 'The other one,' she begged.

'Come for it,' he said, raising his finger away from her body.

Like a dreamer, she lifted her body up to him, till he had sat back on his heels. Her denied breast swung gently, closer, but he had placed the moistened finger on one knee.

'Here,' he said.

And the sight of his masculinity stopped her.

'Don't be afraid, Eve,' he whispered. His hand took hers and laid it against his thigh and as she felt his surging strength, he shuddered. 'I wonder if you have any idea,' he groaned, 'what is happening inside my body! And,' he added, more softly, 'what is happening within my heart.'

A wanton surge flooded through Eve's body, unleashing all inhibitions. Now, her need was too great to be shy. Gently she stroked his body, watching his half-closed eyes and tossing head as he struggled to control the level of pleasure she was giving him.

Boldly she wrapped her legs around his hips, bringing her breasts to rub lightly against his heaving chest. Matt fiercely ground his mouth into hers in a frenetic bid to pacify her.

She began to fight for what she wanted, to moan and plead, not caring who heard or who came in, nor that she had long abandoned all pride. Her senses seemed to have left her and only sensation remained. He was the devil,

the very devil himself, and she was his captive, body and
soul.

'You do need me, don't you,' he muttered.

She nodded, unable to speak.

'Sweetheart. You must admit that you can't leave.
I ...'

Eve closed her eyes in pain. All this, so that he could
get his own way! He'd *said* he'd do anything ... It chilled
her ardour, a cold moment of rationality flashing through
her head like a harsh, purifying laser, burning out the
madness.

'Leave me alone!' she cried. 'You see, I know I need
you, I want you, but it's only my body, Matt! My body
is taking over my brain and I don't like it! Please, I
daren't ...'

Her voice trailed away to a whisper.

'You don't trust me yet. Oh, Eve, how can you do this
to me! You're asking the impossible. I can't ... Damn
you! You *will* ask for me. But not this time. This time, I
will show you what longing is, what real emptiness can
be. I will *make* you take a decision about me; you've
given me so little time to persuade you that this is a lifetime affair, and I must *make* you see what's in your
stubborn, self-effacing heart. You love me, Eve Foster,
as I love you, and by the time this night is ended, you'll
admit it and come willingly to me!'

Matt pushed her to the mattress and his weight
covered her. His gentle fingers trailed slowly down her
body and he pushed aside her traitorously willing legs
with one knee. Then Eve experienced a sensation that
rocketed through her body in a searing flash as his fingers
explored delicately, swiftly finding the most sensitive
part of her body. She arched and moaned under the

rhythm of his thumb as it drew wave after wave of exquisite pleasure through every nerve, aware that he was soothing her with his voice, a voice which cracked huskily in her ear. She had no idea what was happening, or what was to happen. No man had ever touched her, or opened her up like a flower.

Matt's head bent and she was stunned by the warm moist cavity of his mouth and the final, supremely erotic touch of his tongue. It drifted, curled, twisted and tantalised till her delirium took on a deeper keening and she was no longer aware of him, only the rising upsurge of stimulation centred within her womb which promised more unearthly pleasures.

She was still denied him. And her long-frustrated body burst asunder in a series of rippling nerves, driven insane by Matt's sensitising fingers, reaching its climax alone. As she lay there, shuddering helplessly, bewildered and emotionally aching for him still, he kissed her brutally, his face a mask of tension. Then he picked up his clothes, dressed rapidly and left.

Eve's body wouldn't stop shaking. It trembled from head to foot. Yet physically she was satiated and she slept, better than she had for a long time. Though when she woke, her body still quivered and she felt as though she would never stand on her legs, they were so weak.

It was five o'clock. She had wasted her last afternoon. Wasted? Maybe she had found out just how far Matt would go to get what he wanted. So far, but not far enough, she groaned. For the longing had surged back at the thought of him.

He had purposely worked on her like a man promising a child a great treat. He had beckoned her to a table, eased her starvation with an appetiser and deliberately refused her the feast. It had been done with great, calculated skill, perfectly timed—the timing of long experience. Matt Cavell was a true sophisticate and a ruthless one. He would do anything to get what he wanted and she was in his sights as a malleable, suitable woman for him and his daughter.

Where was the love? He had declared it, but all he'd shown was need. She was well qualified, professionally and emotionally, for being a companion, after all, and he was no fool.

The bastard! He *knew* she wanted to stay, *knew* her passion for him had strung her self-esteem so fine that it stretched like gossamer. Yet she could not, would not, walk out on her obligation. If Matt Cavell *really* wanted her, he would have to wait a long time.

Matt. His name, every movement of his body, the man-smell of him, the taste of the salt on his skin, the smooth silk of his shoulders and the power within them, filled her thoughts, excluding all else, clamouring one message over and over again. Obsession.

She was totally mortified. It must be that she was old and desperate. A feeling of cheapness and humiliation deepened as gradually her conscious mind focused on a great deal of noise in the villa. Reluctant to face Matt again after her embarrassing capitulation and his calm control, she listened at the door.

It sounded as though he was barking orders and Dodi was squawking somewhere in the kitchen. What was going on? She sighed. Nothing those two did would surprise her. Nothing *anyone* did any more would surprise her.

'Come on,' yelled Dodi, outside her door as she banged on it loudly enough to waken any local dead. 'Get up.

Time you got ready.'

Puzzled and resigned—only a few more hours to brave it out, after all—Eve pulled on a simple boot-lace-strapped sundress in the palest mint-green and tried to avoid the wild-eyed hoyden she saw in the mirror. She concentrated on the advice she gave to her students; hold your head up and don't let anyone know you have nerves. They'll believe the image and then, very soon, so will you.

The corridor was buzzing with efficient looking Spaniards in white coats, carrying trays and boxes. On the patio, she found Matt and Dodi with their arms affectionately around each other's shoulders, supervising the fixing of arc lights.

Matt eyed her contemplatively; she gave a brief smile and gripped the back of a chair tightly.

'Look, look,' squealed Dodi when she saw Eve. 'Isn't it fun?'

'Er, yes, lots of fun,' she said warily.

'Silly! Haven't you guessed? Matt is giving us a party.'

'Us?'

'Mmm. You and me. His girls, he says.'

'His . . .' Eve's mouth firmed and she made sure she didn't catch his glance.

'Heavenly, it's going to be heavenly,' gurgled Dodi, very much in her element, as she darted from one workman to another, getting in their way and extending the time it took for them to complete their jobs.

'It's a farewell party,' said Matt.

'Really,' she said in a flat voice.

'You might be more enthusiastic. Dodi's full of it,' he said.

'Damn Dodi!' she hissed.

'Oh Eve, you're wonderful,' he grinned.

'Stop treating me like—like . . .'

'I adore you. Hadn't you noticed?' he asked softly. 'I've treated you like a woman. Don't you like that? I can't keep my hands off you, and I'm trying to desperately. Eve, I'm trying to be honourable towards you, but it's hellish hard. Help me!'

A deep red flush stained her face and fled over her body.

'Tonight is going to be very special,' he began.

'Oh, God!' she breathed, unable to bear his eyes raking her body. Ridiculous that mere eyes could set her aflame.

'Your friends are all coming, and loads of people from the beach and the hotel. You can't *not* be there.'

'This is the last time you back me into a corner, do you hear?' she grated.

'Oh, I intend to have you in quite a few corners,' he promised. 'All the days of your life.'

The image of them both, pressed intimately against a wall, hurtled in violent waves through her bones.

'I go tomorrow,' she breathed.

'Of course,' he said as if patronising a child.

'I mean it!'

'Of course you do,' he grinned.

'Yes, Matt!' she yelled and cracked one hand across his face, running into her room and slamming the door.

Hardly able to believe that she had created such a public scene, Eve leaned against the panels and tried to calm her breathing. He was playing with her, as a cat plays with a mouse. But she wouldn't give in again. For the sake of her friends and appearances, she would attend this party. But tonight she'd sleep at the hotel, even if she had to spend all night in the lounge! Then only a few hours and she would be leaving this island and Matt for good.

That thought gave her no consolation. A wicked desire to demand the payment of his body nagged away. It would be a shame if she left without tasting the pleasure his body could undoubtedly give. Yet once home, she would regret it for evermore. Her own self-respect was vital to her, however much she continually forgot that fact whenever Matt touched her.

At eight, she was startled to catch Dodi clambering in through her bedroom window. Dodi giggled at her surprise and put a finger to her lips.

'Don't tell Matt, he'll be furious. He'd have a fit if he knew I'd been staggering along ledges ten feet up.'

'There is a door,' pointed out Eve quietly.

'He said you wouldn't open it. You should see his face! He's been in a storming fury for the last few hours! Your finger marks are only just wearing off. I offered him some of my make-up but he threw me out. Literally threw me out,' she said rubbing a bruised arm. 'What did he do? Did he try to kiss you?' she asked breathlessly.

'Why don't you ask him?' suggested Eve sharply.

'I did! He said, "Shut up, Dodi, and mind your own damn business." Just like that. All growly. I do hope you'll let him kiss you,' she said wistfully. 'That would be divine.'

'Hardly divine,' said Eve wryly. 'My dear girl, it would be ridiculous.'

'That's stuffy. No wonder he's cross with you. All this tension is so exciting. You've really shaken him! Isn't it fun!'

'Your idea of fun and mine aren't the same,' observed Eve, turning to the three dresses on the bed.

'No, I've noticed,' said Dodi kindly. 'Never mind. I expect I'll be like you when I'm your age.'

'Never!' grinned Eve.

'That's better! I'm glad you're over your temper now. Matt will be pleased. What are you wearing?'

'I don't know.' She held up one, then the others against her. 'It doesn't really matter. I'm not sure why I'm dithering.'

'I know why. And it does matter,' insisted Dodi. 'That's awful,' she said frankly. 'Boring. Try that one, the pale blue job. No, don't put a bra on! That's dullsville.'

'I am dullsville, remember?' murmured Eve, piqued. 'Anyway, I can't get away with not wearing a bra. I'm too big.'

'You're gorgeous. Matt says you're built like a Venus. I suppose he ought to know?'

'Dodi!' scolded Eve, blushing furiously. Had he discussed her with his daughter?! She would never get used to his casual attitude towards sex.

'Well, I think you've got lovely breasts,' pursued Dodi. 'Go on, try wearing the dress with just briefs underneath. If it were me, I wouldn't bother with them either,' she said saucily.

'*You* are going to lead your father a right dance,' muttered Eve as she struggled into the soft folds of the thin dress.

'Not half as much as the one you're leading him,' grinned Dodi.

'Me? I'm not leading him any dance!' protested Eve.

'Huh! Oh, that's lovely,' the girl rattled on, distracted by Eve's image in the mirror. 'You look scrummy. All the men will eat you up. Don't know why we bothered with grub.'

Eve grinned in despair and shook her head, then found herself mesmerised by her reflection.

'See? Now everyone will know what a great shape you are,' said Dodi smugly.

'It's . . . it's a bit too revealing,' demurred Eve, pulling the neckline higher. Without a bra, her breasts hung unconfined and drew the deep scoop further over her pale golden contours. A deep cleavage shimmered invitingly as she moved this way and that, the soft mounds of her breasts gently shifting. 'I *can't* wear this! It's outrageous!'

''Course you can. Crack their eyeballs,' grinned Dodi.

She had no wish to crack anyone's eyeballs. Eve paused, in the act of unzipping the back fastener. Perhaps . . . Dammit, she was fed up with being Aunty Eve. Tonight, for this one night of her life, she would find out what it was like to . . . crack eyeballs.

'What are you doing!' wailed Dodi, as Eve lifted out a pair of low sandals. 'You're not wearing *those*!' she scorned, darting to the door and unlocking it. 'Wait,' she promised mysteriously.

Left alone, Eve practised moving in the dress, watching the mirror to see what happened, awed to see how provocative she looked.

'Here!' Dodi rushed in, quite breathless, thrust a pair of teetering high stilettoes on to Eve's bare feet and dragged her out, not giving her a chance to see what effect they had.

If she had known she would never have made her entrance. The shoes had thrown her weight forwards and gave her a wiggle to her walk which she had never had before. Her eyes gleamed softly with nervous anticipation and heightened fever. As she was led to the patio by Dodi, she felt people either side of her catch their breath.

Matt turned in her direction and stared. Eve was nervously running her tongue over her full coral lips. His jaw dropped for a moment, then he snapped his mouth shut and thrust his glass at somebody.

'Good heavens! What are you up to?' he hissed in Eve's ear.

'Up to? I've come to the party,' she said coolly. 'Like you said. Hello, Mrs Walker, I do like you hair. What do you think of the lights—aren't they pretty?'

She had shouldered him away and he could hardly accost her now she was surrounded by the guests from the hotel.

'Dance with me, Eve, you've got to dance with me,' said one of the young men, mesmerised.

'No. She dances with me,' came Matt's stern voice. A strong arm yanked her into his body and they were locked in a tight embrace, shuffling to slow sense-evoking love songs. Eve's intention melted in his arms. Her bones dissolved in his warmth. She kept her eyes lowered, to hide her reactions.

'Poor Eve,' he muttered into her hair as he held her close. 'I've gone too far.'

'That's true,' she said tartly.

Too far! Not far enough, she thought grimly. It might have been further than he had intended, more than he had wanted to do, but she wanted more.

'What made you wear this dress?' he asked.

'I've worn it before,' she said crossly.

'Not exactly like that,' he said gently.

'Don't you like it?'

'No.'

'Everyone else does.'

'They're ogling you. Is that what you want?'

She clung to him, as if he would hide her embarrassment. All she had wanted was for him to desire her, to see what he's missed. It had been a stupid, immature gesture. She should never have listened to Dodi!

'It's too late to change now, mermaid,' he said. 'You'll have to brazen it out. And brazen is the word,' he said wryly. 'Have a good time.'

He led her to where Mrs Thomas and family stood and, lightly kissing Eve's fingertips, abandoned her.

There was a vaguely dignified scramble as partners moved in her direction, and she was swept on to the floor in triumph by the winner. Eve succumbed to a whole new experience. It seemed many men there found her attractive, even if Matt didn't. It was, however, an empty victory.

Her glance flashed to Matt, standing by the edge of the window-opening. Beside him was a young girl from the hotel, a sixteen-year-old. Her parents were seething quietly in the background, as his lazy eyes smiled at her and she raised her little face to his in awe and adoration.

Eve was furiously jealous, the hard pangs of hatred burning like a canker. Matt glanced casually up and caught her eye. His wicked lips curved in a mocking grin.

Then the low growl of a guitar throbbed through the still night and the spine-tingling sound of a flamenco rent the air. Through the dancing couples, gipsies stamped arrogantly on to the patio; not the usual sanitised tourist dancers, but rough field gipsies, faces harsh and seared with work, and black raging fire in their eyes.

Eve felt the throb driving into her veins. Without looking, she knew Matt's eyes were on her and she quivered. The male dancer postured and curved around the woman who strutted seductively, her eyes lowered in demure pretence, hiding flaring passion as the man caressed her with every twist of his body.

Helpless to stop herself, Eve slanted a glance at Matt. His lips had parted in desire—or was he acting again? It had the right effect, anyway, her breasts surged in that frighteningly independent way they had of betraying the state of her body. She tensed more and more as the music slipped into a faster, wilder tempo and the dancer whirled violently, hurtled by the searing cacophony of sound into a frenzied climax which ended in a startling flurry of arching bodies and dominating male virility, filling Eve with its raw passion.

For several minutes, the clapping washed over her in a blur, while a tropical heat poured into her empty, longing loins. Then, in the ensuing mêlée, she quickly left the room and hurried blindly along dark corridors, not knowing what she was doing or where she was going, only that this was some kind of escape. There was a sound behind her; turning, she saw Matt's menacing figure blocking a door, his shoulders visibly rising and falling.

'Come. I'll give you your wages,' he said with a growl.

'Where?' she asked cautiously.

He gave a sigh of exasperation. 'Do you want your money or don't you?' He swung around and she had no choice but to follow him.

They entered a brightly lit room: his study. Eve's face dropped. So much for enticing him, she thought bleakly. He was going to pay her off and find someone else to play mother to Dodi.

'If you'll sign here?'

She stalked over to the desk. Matt closed in on her and

she scrawled her signature hastily, unable to bear being with him a moment longer.

'And here.'

His arm stretched across her, suffocating her body with the warm tang that drifted to her nostrils as he moved. To her fury, her hand was shaking uncontrollably and she had to stop for a moment before finishing the signature.

A wad of money was placed in her hand.

'Right, that's all,' said Matt. 'Unless you had anything else in mind?'

Glaring, she moved to the door.

'I might not see you again,' she said coldly. 'I'll make sure I say goodbye to Dodi before she goes to bed, but I'll make my goodbyes to you now.'

Eve planned to convince Dodi that she would keep in touch with her after she had left. It was bad enough abandoning the child to Matt's erratic fathering, let alone break the first deep friendship the girl had made. She would miss Dodi, very much. And Matt.

'I'll see you at breakfast,' he said.

'Oh, no. I'm spending tonight at the hotel,' she said in triumph. 'I've finished my job and been paid.'

'Look at your contract, mermaid,' he said smugly. 'You've signed to stay here one more night.'

'Oh, you . . .! Then you can have your money back,' she cried.

'You'll still be breaking your contract. And I can enforce it.' His eyes burned furiously. He looked angry enough for anything.

'You . . .!'

'Gently, mermaid,' he smiled.

'Stop it! I'm not a stupid mermaid!' she raged. 'Now I

know how you get your own way in your job; you're
utterly ruthless. For you, the end justifies the means.
Well, some people aren't prepared to live that kind of
dishonour.'

'Nevertheless, I win,' he said easily.

'Not exactly,' she said, tilting her head up. 'You tried
every trick in the book to get me to stay and act as your
daughter's chaperon and pacifier. But I'm going home
tomorrow.'

'Are you?' he raised one eyebrow.

'Yes,' she cried.

'I don't think so,' he said, moving forwards. 'You need
me too much. And I need you.'

Dodi's voice could be heard calling.

Eve stared long and hard at Matt. He seemed so sure of
her and she hated that.

'Whoops, sorry.' Dodi had skidded into the room,
swerved and was about to hurry out again.

'Wait! I'm coming,' said Eve. 'I think I'll dance all
night.'

'Oh goodie! Come on Matt,' Dodie said happily.

'I'll follow you in a moment,' he said softly. 'I need a
few minutes to myself.'

During the next two hours, Matt did everything he
could to tantalise Eve, and she was furious at his callous,
selfish methods. He seemed to take a perverse delight in
brushing against her, throwing her sultry glances,
igniting her with an accidental grazing of his thigh, or the
touch of his hand. Whatever she did; dancing, eating,
wandering about the patio or lounge, he was there,
hovering, forcing her to acknowledge his charismatic
presence, flaunting the fact that she could not, would
never, forget him. Her nerves were in shreds. Her body

was rising to a heat which she couldn't quieten.

The guests gradually left. Listlessly, no longer keeping up any pretence of gaiety, she slumped into an easy-chair and kicked off her shoes.

'Shall I massage those little feet of yours?' asked Matt innocently.

'No!' She tucked them under her crossly.

'You'd better go to bed, Dodi,' said Matt.

'I don't—oh. Yes. Goodnight, Eve.' She put her arms around Eve's neck and hugged her tightly. 'I do love you so much,' she whispered.' ''Night Matt,' she said, pretending to eat Matt's neck.

''Night, my darling,' he smiled.

'I'm going too,' said Eve, not wanting to be alone with Matt.

'Not yet. I have a proposition to make.'

'I'm going to bed,' she said firmly.

'Afraid?' he mocked.

'Of course not,' she defied.

'Then listen.'

Pouting a little, Eve lay back gracefully in the chair, trying to look casual.

'You don't want to go and neither Dodi nor I want you to leave,' he began smoothly.

'I have to,' she said stubbornly, her stomach hollowing into an aching void.

'I'd like you to be a permanent member of the family.'

That was a come-down from a member of his team! He obviously felt she was more suited to be this wretched nanny. 'Oh, no. I'm not working as a companion for ever. That's a waste of my qualifications. I'm sorry if that's the idea you've been cherishing, but you don't seem to realise that my career is very important. And I can't break my contract at the college, anyway. I have to give a term's notice at least and even then I'd leave them with problems of continuity. Don't you understand how vital it is that my groups have security? I'm honour-bound to return next week.'

'Eve,' he said rising, his eyes aflame.

'No!' she cried, backing away. 'Don't start your wily seduction scene, it won't work. I have a contract to fulfil and I can't renege on it, even if I wanted to. I won't stay.'

'Not even as my wife?' he asked softly.

Eve was stupefied. Then it dawned on her. This was his final sacrifice to the altar of convenience. To offer his 'model of womanhood' to his daughter, he was even prepared to marry.

'You bastard!' she whispered. 'That's a loathsome way to entice me! You know I'm virtually on the shelf——'

'Tell that to the men present tonight,' he growled.

'That wasn't me and you know it. You're playing on the emotions of a potential spinster with a heart of gold. Well, I'm fed up with that image. I've discovered that inside me there's a heart of pure steel. I will not be married to you just because you find it convenient.'

'Eve!'

'Don't come near me!' she spat in contempt. 'I wouldn't have you if you offered me the whole of this island as a bribe! I have principles, some standards. From the moment I saw you, you turned my life into a grovelling abandon to the baser instincts. You're destruction, Matt. I don't like what I've become under . . . under your hands. I'm sorry for you and Dodi but I will not allow myself to be completely destroyed by you. For, by heaven, if I married you, I would be!'

'But I thought——'

'Yes, I'm sure you did,' she said scornfully. 'Don't mistake the immature fumblings of a mesmerised virgin for love, Matt. There's an element of hero-worship, sure, but in the cold light of day you just don't measure up to offer enough in compensation for that kind of marriage.'

'And who will, Eve? What sort of man do you want?'

'I don't know. I'm not sure there is one,' she said quietly. 'All I know is, you're not it!'

'I should have taken you when I had the chance,' he said bitterly. 'All my life I'll regret that.'

'I'm sure you will,' she said sharply. 'It would have been wise to strike while the iron was hot.'

'Iron?' he queried, his gaze raking her body. 'There's too much melting softness there for any iron.'

Once again, he had crushed her bones with a glance.

'In your arms, Eve,' he said in his deep, rich voice, pressing home his unexpected advantage, 'I am healed. You . . .'

'I know. I soothe you. Very nice. It's cheaper than tranquillisers, isn't it, and not half as habit-forming.' She glared. 'You have a choice, Matt. Leave me alone and I won't create a stormy leavetaking for Dodi's sake, or I go to the Molins now and don't see either of you again. Which is it to be?'

'Come on, Eve, you don't want to go. We have a lifetime together.' He moved closer and she backed away angrily.

'Give up,' she said harshly, the thumping in her chest rising to a tumult. 'Polite and courteous goodbyes tomorrow morning—after leaving me alone all night—or I leave now.' She would *not* have a loveless marriage just so that Matt Cavell could jet off all round the world, knowing that Dodi was in good hands!

'I don't believe it,' he whispered.

'No? Well, I rarely dig my heels in, but when I do, I'm immovable. Especially where my conscience, my heart, and my honour is concerned. I have a conscience about leaving my employers and those teenagers in the lurch,' she rapped. 'I grew very fond of them over the last year and I care about their future.'

'And us? Aren't you ... fond of us, don't you care about our future?'

She stared at him for one long minute, then, unable to reply, torn between two powerful contenders for her heart, she spun on her heel. 'I'm leaving tonight,' she said tightly.

For a moment, Eve was distracted by a sound outside the door and light, running feet. But Matt hadn't heard, and it must have been a trick of her imagination. He had caught her arm and drawn close.

'Don't. I admit temporary defeat. I'll leave you alone. I have been waiting for you all my life; I can wait a little longer if I have to. But hear this; at the end of your college year, I will come for you, ready or not. And I'll take you with me if I have to abduct you. In the morning, we'll talk properly about this. I have nothing left at the moment.'

Lines of exhaustion dragged at his face. He looked like she felt.

'Be there in the morning, to say goodbye,' he pleaded.

'Very well,' she said coldly, and walked out on him.

That time came slowly for Eve. Dodi hadn't answered her soft knock on the door—she was obviously asleep and their talk would have to wait till the morning. Maybe then she could offer Dodi a place to stay, if she decided on taking up the Nursery Nursing course. She watched the dark turn to twilight, then a dull yellow filtered into the sky and golden shafts suffused the cheerless room. Everything was packed; her belongings and memories which she had spread around her so happily, ready now for her return journey.

She forced a little breakfast down, sitting with a silent Matt. Dodi didn't appear. Finally, she had to speak.

'Shall I wake her? I've only half an hour before I leave for the airport,' asked Eve, anxiously.

She wanted some time to speak quietly to Dodi before she left. It was bad enough eating breakfast with an icily taciturn Matt, let alone having to rush her last few moments.

Matt was obviously worried about how he would handle the future with his daughter. His face looked drawn and grey and his eyes were bloodshot as though he had hardly slept either.

'I'll go and get her up,' he said wearily.

Eve followed him with her soft grey eyes. Every line of his body she memorised, storing away the images for ever in vivid memory, forcing away the sick feeling in the pit of her stomach. She must keep her head. He would use any weakness to his advantage and she refused to allow him to use her.

Then there came a shout from Matt, a desperate, despairing cry. Eve flung down her napkin and ran to Dodi's bedroom.

'What is it?' she cried at Matt's crumpled body, huddling on the bed.

'She's gone!' he grated.

Eve took one look at the empty, unused bed and plucked a note from his nerveless fingers.

'Run away?' Eve's eyes rounded. 'She never thought

I'd actually go and . . . Oh Matt! How could she!' Dodi
must have been listening last night! What had they said?
Eve racked her brains, fighting down the overpowering
feeling that she was responsible for all this. She should
have gone to Dodi and explained, been totally honest,
appealed to her to understand her predicament.

'What do you mean?' he yelled, rounding on her. 'She
loved you! The one woman who gave her love,
undemanding, unconditional love, and you have to
abandon her! She cares for you as . . . Dammit, Eve! It's
all your fault! We both were convinced you'd stay and it's
only your damn stubborn principles that made you so
determined to leave!'

'You were convinced?' said Eve incredulously, distracted from his hurtfully true words.

'Of course. Why do you think neither of us was
particularly upset that you were about to go? I thought
. . . I thought I could persuade you to stay. I was sure of it.
Not until the very last minute did I ever imagine you'd
turn your back on us. And now,' he said bitterly, 'now
this is a direct result of your decision.'

He didn't have to voice her thoughts! Surely he must
realise that Dodi's disappearance had upset her too? And
he had been equally responsible for the situation.

'Oh! How can you be so cruel! That's a beastly, hurtful
thing to say. You know how fond I am of Dodi. I can't
help my commitments: we all knew them when I took on
this job. Besides,' she said, suddenly suspicious, 'how do I
know that you haven't both arranged this between you?'

'My God!' he breathed. 'For a sweet-natured woman
you certainly have some bad opinions of people
sometimes! Do I look as though I knew this was
happening?'

'Anything wrong, sir?' Frank's face had appeared at the doorway.

'Yes, everything,' he said tersely. 'Dodi has run away.' He leaned against the wall, looking haggard in the morning sun. 'You'd better leave the police to me. I'll ring them now. In the meantime, Eve, perhaps you'd think of some of the places she might have bolted to.'

Wordlessly she nodded, realising from his response that he hadn't arranged this drama at all. Sick inside, she brought her mind to bear on the problem and had a list of possible refuges when he returned.

'I've alerted the airport and the port authorities,' he said.

'Mrs Turner says she's taken her passport and money,' said Eve anxiously, worried at the evident strain on his face.

'Right. Now she's to stay here in case there are any developments, and to hand over photographs of Dodi to the police when they arrive. I've told the Inspector that I have no intention of waiting for them and that I intend to start searching.'

'What about me?' asked Eve anxiously.

'You!' He shook her shoulders, his furious face inches away. 'You stay, of course!'

'My plane——!'

'Will leave without you,' he finished grimly.

'You can't make me stay,' she began frantically.

'Don't bet on that,' he scalded. 'I know that your honour,' his voice curled scornfully over the word, 'means more to you than I do. But you can damn well meet your obligations to Dodi—it's your fault she's disappeared!'

'That's grossly unfair! It's *not* my fault!'

'Get some things ready for a long day out,' he said curtly. 'We have one hell of a task ahead.'

They stared angrily at each other, unlike the lovers they had so nearly been. Eve gave a helpless gesture, knowing he was right and hating him for that. He was affecting her life *again*!

While Matt sourly gave orders for a packed lunch, Eve quickly checked her diary for the home number of the Head of her Technical College.

'You can't let us down, Eve,' he remonstrated. 'We've one hundred and thirty applicants to get through.'

'I'm aware of that, John,' she said. 'But Doug could start on those. He's taken over before, when I've been ill.'

'Not for interviews. You know that you're the only one who can rank their needs,' he replied in an exasperated tone. 'And you'll be the one working with them—what's the point of someone else arranging the groups if they don't gel with you?'

'I'm sorry, I really am. I wouldn't be doing this if it wasn't an emergency. Please manage as well as you can. I doubt I'll be stuck here for long. A day or so at the most.'

'Make sure that's all it is,' warned the Head. 'I'm relying on you. If you don't make those interviews, we may have to abandon that particular course.'

Eve's stomach turned over. 'Don't do that. I'll get back, I'll really try.'

'You must do better than that, you *have* to get back. Those kids need you Eve, remember that.'

'I *know*!' she yelled, suddenly at the end of her tether. 'Everyone needs me! You all lean on me and I can't stand it any more! I haven't had any peace this holiday and you're expecting me to start up as if I'd had a long rest! I wish you'd all leave me alone for once and stop making demands all the time!'

Angrily she banged down the phone, collapsing shakily into a chair when she discovered her legs would no longer hold her.

'Are you ready?'

She jumped at Matt's icy tones.

'Pull yourself together,' he said distantly. 'It's no good either of us being in a state. We must remain calm.'

'*Calm*!' she flared, gripping the sides of the chair in fury. She didn't trust her legs sufficiently to stand. 'You and your daughter create merry hell in my life and you expect me to stay calm while everything tumbles about me in ruins? *Ohh*!'

'That kind of reaction isn't helping,' he said tightly.

'Maybe not, but it stops me from doing what I'd like to, and that, if you want to know, is to thump you good and hard!'

'We're leaving,' he said in a threatening tone.

With a tightening of her lips, Eve rose unsteadily and collected a light jacket and her handbag from her room. Matt was revving up the car impatiently when she joined him and they swept out of the drive before she had even slammed the passenger door.

That day was a nightmare, one she would never in her life forget. They visited every place on the route to Valldemossa and the little secret bay, stopping, it seemed, at any likely hotel, taverna or bar where Dodi might be staying. No one had seen her.

Throughout the tiring journey, Matt had not spoken to her, but stormed in and out of the car, becoming increasingly agitated as night fell and they had still found no sign of his daughter. Three times he rang his villa and three times Mrs Turner told him that she had no news either.

'We ought to return,' ventured Eve nervously, discovering it was now ten o'clock.

Despondently, Matt turned the car for Cala San Vicente. When they arrived, he went to find out what the police had done and Eve was left to eat supper on her own. For one brief moment, she contemplated calling a taxi and leaving, sick as she was with the whole affair. But she couldn't. She had to know whether Dodi was all right or had come to harm. The girl was such a flirt, anything could have happened. She began to worry that she had become mixed up with a gang of boys and was reaping the results of her provocative behaviour.

As the days passed, the police slackened their efforts, shrugging their shoulders and saying that many girls went missing and Dodi hadn't actually left the island. They implied she was probably with a secret boyfriend.

Matt haunted bars and discos every night, snatching only a couple of hours' sleep before doggedly setting off to search the next morning. It wrenched Eve's heart to see him so utterly dejected and eking out such a miserable existence.

Then, a telephone call one morning changed everything. Matt's response to the speaker was electrifying.

'Eve!' he shouted, his eyes a glittering madness. 'Honorio thinks he saw Dodi!'

'Where?' Eve grabbed his hands in excitement.

'In Puerto Pollença this morning! He was buying fish in the market. He's *sure* it was her! He started to run towards her but she disappeared. Oh, Eve, I can't believe it!'

'Matt, it's wonderful news. Did he say how she looked,

was she all right, was she with someone else?'

'Um, I didn't ask. I was too stunned.' He grinned, and Eve was pained by that grin, for it brought him alive again, once more a devastatingly attractive, confident man.

'Well, what are we waiting for!' she laughed, setting her eyes dancing.

Matt swung her around and hugged her. 'Be practical, Eve. Have something to eat. It could be a long search. We've already combed the Puerto once.'

She sobered immediately. 'Should we alert the police?'

'Yes. I'll ring. We'll get Frank to come with us and make out a plan of campaign over breakfast.'

'I couldn't eat a thing!'

'You must,' he scolded, laughing. 'Force it down. I'm going to.'

Their search of the port drew a blank. But there was hope—and the knowledge that Dodi was alive and well.

'The little scallywag,' muttered Matt as they slid into the car for the homeward journey that evening, in the half-light. 'When I get hold of her . . .'

'You'll welcome her with open arms and love her and probably shed a tear or two,' said Eve firmly.

'Hmmm. Maybe. At the moment, now I know she's safe, I'm feeling anger.'

'Don't judge. You've no idea what's going on inside that girl.'

'Sweet Eve. What an amazing woman you are.'

She flung him a startled look and heard Frank cough awkwardly in the back. Matt grinned at her and she grinned back, as though they shared a secret.

As they left the outskirts of Puerto Pollença, Eve looked up at the high Sierra which divided the port from the valley of San Vicente. And there, on the right, she was sure she saw a figure in a pair of brief white shorts, long legs striding along what must be a winding road, though it couldn't be seen from where they were.

'Stop!' yelled Eve. That figure had been topped by a head of bouncy yellow curls.

In a reflex action, Matt stopped the car but before it had rolled to a halt, Eve had flung open the door and was racing up the bank to the first level of a road, which obviously led to the main road a little way further on.

'Eve! What the hell are you doing?!'

Unheeding of Matt's shouts, she struggled on, determined to overtake the girl, certain that the image she had seen was really Dodi. Excitement mounted inside her as she ran along the steeply twisting road, her heart pumping hard with the effort. She could hear the heavier tread of the two men behind, and their shouts.

Eve wasn't a natural runner, but that evening it seemed her body had been lent wings. Doggedly she forced her legs to a faster pace. Just above, she was sure she had seen a flash of white. Then she was sure. For above her, just one hairpin bend up, the figure could be seen clearly.

'Dodi! Oh Dodi! It's me, Eve!'

Not wasting any more time, she turned to hurry along the road, but the figure had disappeared. Alarmed that the girl hadn't heard, Eve knew she would never keep up with her if she ran along the road.

She stretched up to the high bank and dug her toes into the scrub. Dust and rocks tumbled around as she grabbed for a handhold.

'Eve! Don't! For God's sake, I don't want you killed!'

Turning slightly, she saw Matt, a few turns of the road below.

Ignoring him, she pulled herself up. Here, the soil was more crumbling than before, less stable. Fewer bushes had formed a network of roots below the surface, holding the dry earth.

Darn! It would have been faster to have run along the road after all.

'Dodi!' she yelled. 'It's all right!'

'Eve, my darling, stop!' yelled Matt, his voice closer now.

Grimly she reached up and gripped a large chunk of white limestone, knowing that Dodi was getting further away. In the distance, she heard a scream and Matt's yell. She looked up. Dodi was stumbling down the bank towards her, setting up a small avalanche of stones which rained all around. Instinctively, Eve pressed herself to the rock, protecting her head with her arms. There was a heavy thud below; the scream had been cut off in mid-air. Dodi lay in an awkward position on the road just below, covered in chalky dust and small stones, a terrible gash in her head.

CHAPTER EIGHT

HALF climbing, half falling, Eve slid down the bank to the unconscious girl. She was about to feel her pulse when Matt came racing up the road, his face distorted in anger.

'Don't touch her!' he yelled.

'I wasn't going to,' began Eve.

Matt thrust her away roughly and knelt down, running a quick eye over his unconscious daughter. He placed two fingers at the angle of her jaw and two on its point and brought her chin forwards and slightly up.

'I could have done that,' accused Eve.

'I'm not used to anyone knowing what they're doing,' he muttered.

'Shall I go for help?' Eve asked timorously.

'Frank has.' Matt touched the scalp gently and parted her hair. 'Hell.'

'What is it?'

'Not sure. Could be a fracture. If it is, it'll be complicated with that bleeding.' He tore off his shirt and held it lightly against her scalp.

'The fall might have injured her spine. How will we get her to the ambulance?'

'Leave it to them. They know how to move people.'

He sounded impatient and angry. 'Don't take it out on me, Matt,' she said quietly.

'Why the hell not?' he growled. 'If you hadn't yelled at her like that and startled her, she would never have fallen.'

'Oh! How can you say that! I . . .' Guilt swamped over her.

'I'm sorry,' he muttered. 'That was uncalled-for. Forgive me. Sit down, you look shocked. Dodi, can you hear me, sweetheart? Listen. You've had a bump on the head. You'll be all right. We'll get you comfortable very soon.'

His voice droned on, soothingly. Eve's legs were shaking, quivering on the warm road. Matt had taken over the situation and she was helpless. It was an odd feeling for her; she was usually the one to whom people turned in a crisis. It unnerved her to be with someone stronger, more capable than herself.

As she watched the two of them together, father and daughter, she felt they were now bonded so closely that no one could come between them. She was nothing in their lives really, other than a glorified babysitter. His attitude now was making that very clear.

For over an hour Eve sat on that road, with Matt speaking constantly in gentle, reassuring tones. He was astounding. Her own legs were stiff and cold. He must be in agony, the way he was crouching, but he gave no sign. And to keep up that continual quiet tone was an amazing achievement—though he was beginning to repeat himself now.

Far in the distance she heard the sounds of an ambulance. Only by a flicker of his eyes did Matt betray he had heard it too, he still continued to talk calmly to Dodi.

The ambulancemen took in the situation at a glance, lifting Dodi with unbelievable care on to the stretcher so that she lay on her stomach. Matt sent Frank back to the villa, bundling Eve into the ambulance.

She watched as the men examined Dodi and Matt

explained what had happened in Spanish. Again she felt
excluded. When Matt had finished, he leaned back, pale
and exhausted, the lines of worry down to his mouth
deeply accentuated.

Eve bit her lip. There was nothing sensible or helpful
that she could say so she stayed silent. But she was aware
of a terrible coldness lying between them; a final
severing of their relationship. She had caused Dodi to
run away—however innocently. She had caused her to
fall. The guilt was mixed with the certain knowledge that
this nightmare holiday would never leave her mind as
long as there was breath in her body.

She began to shake. One of the men placed a blanket
around her shoulders and took her pulse. Her head began
to whirl and she was gently laid down. Feeling a fraud,
she tried to rise when they arrived at the hospital and
Dodi was rushed out, but she was carried in and left on a
trolley.

A long time later she was checked over and pro-
nounced fit—something she knew already—and was at
last allowed to find Matt.

'How is she?' she asked, when she tracked him down
in a cubicle.

'They're operating,' he said harshly.

'Operating?'

His eyes lashed her briefly then he began to pace up
and down rapidly, his chest inflated and his jaw clenched
tightly.

'Matt . . .'

'If only . . .' He stopped.

'What were you going to say?' she asked.

'I have to say it, Eve, it's going round and round my
head like a record, over and over again. This has
happened because of your stupid pride . . .'

'How dare you?' she shouted, amazed at his words. 'I had no pride. If I had, I would never have consented to act as your . . . your *servant* in the first place. It's not a role I'm used to. I'll have you know I'm an independent, highly skilled youth worker. I'm not in the habit of taking on nannying jobs for absentee fathers.'

'By God, Eve, you've got a vicious tongue when you get going! All that veneer of sweetness and light was just a façade, wasn't it?' he sneered. 'Underneath you're as ordinary as everyone else.'

'I never said I wasn't,' she raged.

'No. But I thought you were special. Huh! Is that demure, motherly approach the one you use to get men to fall for you?'

'What are you talking about? I have no "approach". I was just me, till you came along. Ever since I met you, disasters have come my way. You're a walking tempest, Matt Cavell. And let's get one thing straight: I did not flirt with you. I wouldn't know how to.'

'Oh, yes, you did. You made me feel that there could be something between us. All along, you were looking for a bit of fun during your holiday in contrast with your drab life at home. And all along you had your job foremost in your mind.'

'Of course I did! You don't seriously think I was expecting our relationship to be permanent, do you?' she scathed.

Matt swung around and gripped her forearms viciously, his thumbs bruising the skin. 'I thought. Oh, I thought a lot. I had little scenes playing out in my mind.'

'I'm sure,' grated Eve. 'Me at home, patting Dodi on the hand and training her to be docile, while you batted about saving the world.'

'You . . .!' His face was suffused with rage. Then his

hands dropped. 'I want nothing more to do with you, Eve, do you hear? Go back to your teenage drop-outs and act the wonderful earth mother with them. I'm finished with women. My daughter lies in there seriously ill and yet all I can think of is that you are leaving and my heart is being torn apart. I hate myself for it. Hate myself! But by God, you'll leave and get out of my system this minute!'

He was insane, talking nonsense. Eve could hardly understand what he meant.

The door opened. With an exclamation, Matt strode forwards.

'Dodi——'

'Mr Cavell?' The dark-eyed doctor asked sympathetically.

'Yes. Dodi?'

'I am Doctor Perez-Avilla. Your daughter, she has many bruises and many cuts of the body.'

'What about her back? What about her spine?'

'I am telling you, Mr Cavell,' said the doctor patiently. 'We think there is no damage to the spine. Much bruises and swelling. She has a fracture to the skull.'

'Oh, God!' Matt covered his face with his hands.

'That is not a problem, Mr Cavell. The bone will knit together. It is the bleeding that gave a little trouble. We have drawn off the blood and must wait.'

'Can I see her now?' he whispered.

A terrible longing to hold him in her arms swept through Eve. Even worse was the knowledge that he didn't want her to do so.

'You can look through the window, but that is all.'

'Why can't I see her?' he asked desperately.

The doctor regarded him solemnly for a moment. 'The nurses are making her comfortable. Your daughter is in a coma, Mr Cavell. It may take hours before she is herself again, it may be longer.'

'How much longer?' asked Matt in a deadly tone.

Doctor Perez-Avilla shrugged. 'A week, a month, who can say?'

'Let me see her then.' His voice had cracked.

Tears were starting in Eve's eyes. 'What about me?' she began, meaning to say she wanted to see Dodi too.

'*God*!' he growled. 'Go back to the villa and start packing.' He flung a pile of money on to the floor. 'That should be enough for a taxi.'

'No Matt,' she said firmly. 'I can't leave now.'

'Stay, go, do what you like. I honestly don't care at the moment; I've had enough. But I won't have you near. Come within ten yards of me and I'll throw you out myself!'

It was a few days before Dodi was brought back to the villa. Eve hadn't seen Matt at all; he had lived in the waiting-room at the hospital, growing—according to Frank—more and more bitter and irritable as time went by. Dodi's temperature was down and there was no further risk of internal bleeding causing the greatest problem, that of infection. Frank said that the doctors had advised Matt to have his daughter under constant supervision. They had stressed the importance of monitoring the girl unceasingly, and of people she knew well and loved talking to her.

They had discovered where Dodi had stayed; a villager in the mountain village of Es Vila handed in to the police the belongings of a young English girl who had rented a room from him.

Mooning around, Eve rang her parents, explaining that her holiday had been extended, denying with vigour that there would be any problems with the College.

Inside, she didn't feel the same confidence and this was borne out when she finally raised the courage to speak to the Head. Unable to give a definite date when she would return, she was shattered to hear that he was accepting that phone call as her notice. He was not prepared to begin the new term with one tutor for the groups, then switch in mid-stream back to her, it would be too unsettling. And she knew he was right. The situation infuriated her; she had lost her job for nothing. Now even the idea of working for UNDRO was a pipe-dream—with Matt in this angry, resentful mood, she could forget ever working with him. Only the thought that Dodi might need her kept her going.

Mrs Turner had made a bed up in the lounge, on Matt's orders, so that Dodi was surrounded by familiar sounds. Eve watched the ambulance arrive from an upper window. Matt looked terrible. He hadn't shaved at all and his face was grey. Even his movements were listless.

Patiently, she waited, hoping to hear Matt's footsteps coming to his room. He must, she reasoned, want to clean up and rest for a while, then she could go down and take a look at Dodi.

By suppertime, he hadn't appeared, and Eve decided to risk his wrath and go down.

'I thought I told you to stay away,' he growled when he saw her.

'I'm concerned,' she answered quietly.

'So you ought to be. Well, now you're here, you might as well stay with her while I freshen up.' He ran a hand over his emergent beard with distaste. 'If she moves, blinks, so much as quivers a pulse, shout.'

Eve nodded, feeling she had won a small victory of some sort. She gazed sadly at the still girl, looking so sweet and innocent with her halo of baby curls. Some time later, Eve realised she felt stiff and found to her astonishment that it was nearly ten o'clock.

'I'll take over now,' came Matt's hard tones behind her.

Wearily, Eve rose and went to the kitchen. Mrs Turner was just making up two trays.

'Mr Cavell told me to wait supper till he came down,' she said anxiously.

Eve elected to take Matt's tray to him in the lounge. But she found him fast asleep, slumped on the floor, having slipped from the chair without even waking. Asleep, he looked all-in and vulnerable, nothing like the man who had spoken so unreasonably and cruelly before. She picked at her food, then discovered she was ravenous. As night drew on, Eve took to walking around the room in an attempt to stay awake. Frank had suggested he supervised for a while, but Eve had refused.

The sky paled, changed to purple, red and pink, then a deep gold. In her exhaustion, Eve stumbled over Matt's tray on the floor, and he stirred.

'I'm going to bed,' she said quietly.

He glanced at his watch. 'Hell. You've been here all night?'

She nodded. 'There's a salad for you here if you want it. Or I could get you some breakfast.'

'No. Nothing.'

'You must . . .'

'Don't lecture me!' he hissed. 'Go to bed.'

They rarely met after that, each taking turns to watch over Dodi, with Matt refusing to leave her more than was absolutely necessary. It was an uneasy relationship, brought to a head one morning when she walked on to the patio and bumped into Matt. Their fingers touched and locked. For one endless moment, they stayed linked in that way, her eyes focused stupidly on his long tanned fingers which were shooting such warmth into her body. His other hand tipped up her chin and forced her troubled eyes to meet his. Anxiously she searched those lion-flecked lenses, her heart beating so furiously that she thought he must surely reach out and touch it to see if it was really racing at that extraordinary pace. And the thought of his lean fingers touching her breast there made her gasp in shock.

Matt groaned. 'I can't keep my hands off you, do you realise that?' he whispered fervently. 'Do you know I've been fighting all these days to stay calm? My daughter is ill and I should hate you, yet my brain relentlessly drives me to think of you! Oh, Eve!'

His mouth moved over the silk of her hair, brushing lightly, with an indescribable sweetness. Eve pressed slightly against his chest and he released his hold to look down on her. She kept her eyes fixed on the second button of his shirt, noting how the small black hairs on his chest were curling over the white cotton. His bronzed neck rose in a smooth pillar from the open neckline and all she wanted to do was to place her lips at the pulse which was beating so madly.

Matt mumbled into her hair and his lips trailed gently over her temples, her eyes, closed in rapture, down the bridge of her nose, tantalising her by refusing her parted lips.

With a gentle moan, Eve reached around his neck, pushing her fingers through his springing hair, savouring the soft touch of it and the strength of the body drawn tightly against hers. Matt's hands spread flat against her spine, crushing her closer. Now she could feel every part of him. A burning thrilled right through her body as his thighs shifted gently. She caught her breath and tilted her face appealingly to him, spreading her fingers, too, against his head, and bringing his mouth irrevocably down.

'Eve,' he whispered, as their lips quivered, a hair's breadth apart. 'I'm bewitched, dazzled. I can't resist you any longer.'

Then his mouth closed on hers, bruising and punishing in its long-frustrated desire, of pain and agony, devouring every inch till it was totally sensitised. His sharp teeth chewed in maddening sweetness, forcing deep, panting breaths from her body. And he took advantage of her laboured breathing by invading her mouth with the ravishing of his tongue which shocked her with its blatant suggestion, making her pull away to deny him. But he growled in his throat and ran his hands down her back to her hips in fierce possession, setting up a rhythm there that threatened to consume her with hell-fire.

Masterfully, his hands swept up her body, over her hipbones, curving in to enjoy the pleasure of her dipping waist, and spreading slowly up to her breasts. Despite her fighting hands, Matt still was in control of her mouth, still commanding her body. And it was obeying him, completely. She couldn't stop the tide of desire welling up within, the wild recklessness in her head.

'Mmmmm . . .' A gentle murmur—from neither of them!

They paused, shocked into stillness and heard the rustle of bedclothes from the lounge. Dodi!

When they reached her bedside, there was a definite flicker of the child's lashes. Matt and Eve exchanged glances, then he bent down.

'I'm here, sweetheart. Say hello to me,' he murmured.

'Hello,' mumbled Dodi.

Large tears formed in Eve's eyes and furiously she brushed them away. She didn't want to miss anything!

'You're quite safe. At home. I'm here now and I'll take care of you,' continued Matt.

'Eve?' whispered Dodi.

'She's here too,' said Matt. He took Eve's hand and put it in Dodi's. The touch of his fingers had momentarily electrified Eve and she began to tremble at the closeness of his body and the emotional situation.

A beaming smile crossed Dodi's face and she gave a huge sigh, then fell into a deep, normal sleep, her skin now flushed pink and healthy.

'I'm going to bed,' muttered Matt. 'Get Frank to watch over her.'

The anti-climax of it all crushed her. He had reached out for sympathy again! All he had wanted was a sexual release for his tensions and she had been ready to give her love. She couldn't take any more—didn't have to. Now the child was on the way to recovery, there was absolutely no reason for her to stay. Her priorities lay in getting home and finding a job. Desolation swept over her in driving waves. That night, despite a firm resolution not to let the situation get the better of her, she gave in to tears of body-racking intensity. It wasn't like her to cry at all; Matt seemed to have released a dam of emotions that she would rather had been left in their normal, calm pool!

'May I telephone to arrange transport home?' she asked Matt at breakfast the next morning.

'Why?' he said astonished.

'Work,' she said in an emotionless voice.

'But ...' His eyes dropped and he fiddled with his knife. 'Back to your loving students.'

She didn't answer, not wanting to admit that she'd lost

her job. He might offer her the post of companion and she was damned if she would go through all that again! He wouldn't know that it was impossible for her to stay another day with him, loving him as she did, knowing that he was constantly using her.

He seemed to take her silence as confirmation. 'Damn you, Eve! How can you leave me!' he said huskily.

'No problem,' she said casually. 'There's nothing to hold me here. You can manage now—you *must* begin to manage.'

Matt leaned back in his chair, the curve of his mouth tightening and the lines of his face souring. 'Oh, we can *manage*,' he rasped. 'But is that living?'

'I'll ring after breakfast,' said Eve, preoccupied, trying to shut him out, trying to avoid the urge to kiss away the anger on his face.

'I'll do it for you,' he muttered. 'I can probably get you a flight more easily, since I speak the language.'

'Thank you,' she said politely.

'Not at all,' he growled.

That was an awful morning. Confirmation of her 'resignation' came through the post, Dodi didn't want anyone around as she had a headache, and Matt stormed into his study, only to emerge as black as thunder.

'No flights till the morning,' he scowled. 'What are you crying over? What's that, bad news from home?'

He snatched at her letter.

'No! Give it back!' she wailed.

'The College?' he muttered, noticing the letter-head. 'What do they want? Haven't you arranged to delay the courses?'

Eve turned her back on him, her shoulders drooping as she fought for control of the tears. Then, alerted by his silence, she swung round.

'Don't you read my letter!' she cried furiously.

'I couldn't help it,' breathed Matt. 'There was obviously something so wrong ... Eve, why didn't you tell me? This makes a difference!'

'None at all,' she said coldly.

'You can stay,' he said with a flashing grin. 'No sense of honour is making you return now.'

'It's precisely a sense of honour that *is* making me go home,' she said sharply.

'But ...'

'Don't touch me!' she yelled. 'I'm tipping over the edge, do you know that? I've always been so calm and placid and now whenever I'm with you awful things happen and inside my head is wildness and ... and ...' She shook her head to dissipate the thundering rage. 'I can't take any more, Matt,' she whispered dejectedly. 'I refuse to be at your beck and call any more.'

With that, she strode to her room and locked the door, using her time to pack. Later, she went for a walk, and was relieved that Matt had, according to Frank, gone into town. She trudged despondently around the Cala, fixing the images in her mind, for she would never, never come back here again.

She stayed out nearly till suppertime, eating lunch in the local café—though what she ate she couldn't recall. When she returned, she was surprised to see that the table had not been laid on the patio and that Frank and Mrs Turner were bustling around very mysteriously. For a while, she chatted to a sleepy Dodi, then left her to rest. The sun set and Eve sat swinging on the hammock mournfully saying a mental goodbye to the Cala.

Matt tiptoed on to the terrace, shut the doors to the lounge, drew Eve up and took her in his arms.

'Thank you,' he said simply.

That was enough to release the floodgates of Eve's tensions and tattered emotions. With a howl, she buried her head in his shoulder and cried her heart out. He stood there, rocking her, patting her shoulder and murmuring soothing words. Finally, he carried her to a chair and sat her on his knee, holding her close to his broad chest.

'I think you ought to know that I've been making arrangements,' he murmured. 'I'm taking a desk job for a year in London, while Dodi attends a nursing course. I gather it was your idea.'

'Yes. I'm glad.' Now he really didn't need her. A racking sob was wrenched from her body.

'Quietly, mermaid,' he said attempting to wipe her eyes. 'Time to return to the Deep.'

'What?' She struggled ineffectually.

'Supper. A waterside one. Though you seem to have provided a lot of salt water already.'

Through her tears, she smiled. A last dinner with him would be heavenly, something to treasure.

With a breathtakingly swift gesture, he swept her up and strode down the steps as though she weighed nothing at all. Stopping her protests and questions with a secretive grin, he made his way to the deserted beach. There in the darkness, was a small rowing-boat. Without explanation, he dropped her on to its seat and was wading into the gentle surf, pushing the boat out to sea.

'Matt! What on earth are you doing!' she said, horrified.

'Wait and see,' he said smugly.

'No, you . . .' As she stood, the boat rocked alarmingly.

'I'm in no mood for arguments,' he rasped, his eyes starkly white in the darkness. 'You said you couldn't take any more; well, neither can I. You've dissembled long enough. Sit down and be quiet.'

Trembling, Eve obeyed as he rowed out, the oars dipping silkily in the black water. Again, he was leading her to the little cove next to the Cala. What was he doing?

As the boat turned around the small headland, an astonishing scene met Eve's eyes. So astonishing, that she knew she was in a dream. The cove was lit by guttering oil lamps, resting precariously in rock crevices. On the minute beach stood two chairs and a small table, spread with a snowy linen cloth. And there, standing sentinel over a champagne bucket, was Frank.

Madness. Utter, surrealistic madness.

Her widened eyes turned to Matt.

'Out you get,' he said, as though they were on a Thames outing.

She did, giggling.

'Evening, miss,' said Frank, barely concealing a grin.

'Frank . . .'

'Shall I open the champagne now, sir?' he asked deferentially.

'Er . . . yes, I think so. Then perhaps you'd leave. I think we have all we need.'

'I'm sure you do, sir,' agreed Frank. The soft whoosh of gas was expelled from the bottle and a faint haze appeared at its neck. Eve was directed to a chair and her glass filled. Frank, his role completed, rowed away silently.

'Do you like lobster vol-au-vents?' asked Matt coolly.

'Do I like . . .!'

'They're still hot,' he said with satisfaction, serving her from a covered dish. 'We timed that well.'

'But . . .'

'Eat up. Talk later. If you must,' he added.

A bewildered Eve silently ate the pastries. The corners of her mouth began to turn up as Matt solemnly dished up cold baby *poussin* and tiny minted potatoes.

'Matt, this is ridiculous!' she laughed.

'Isn't it?' he said, calmly dissecting the chicken. He caught her eye and began to grin, then they were both laughing till the tears came.

'If anyone should see . . .' gasped Eve.

'They'd never believe it. It's just too silly for words!' laughed Matt.

'Can you imagine, a party of tourists motoring past this cove . . .'

'Goggling at two idiots having a stately dinner in the middle of nowhere . . .'

'It's an advert,' said Eve firmly. 'You're having this filmed.'

'Damn! You've guessed! OK, folks,' yelled Matt to the silent cliff above. 'It's a wrap. Go home. We might as well have the melon and strawberries,' he said in a conversational tone. 'The advertisers are paying, after all.'

'Idiot,' laughed Eve. 'It's not a dream, is it?' she asked breathlessly.

'Could be,' said Matt cheerfully.

'What *is* all this about?'

'Moonlit supper. Well, oil-lit. I couldn't arrange the moon,' he said, gazing at the black velvet sky.

'Look I appreciate all the trouble that Mrs Turner—and Frank—have gone to, but . . .'

Matt broke in, looking pained. 'I did it,' he said. 'I did it all. Every strawberry hand-picked in the market. The vol-au-vent cases were from a packet,' he said apologetically, 'but I did watch them in the oven. Er . . . you don't think there was too much marjoram on the chicken, do you?'

Eve was speechless. He'd done all this? Her hear

began to pound. He'd done all this for her.

'No? Good. Have some more champagne.'

'Oh, Matt!'

'Ah,' he grinned, his devil's lips curving in sensuality.
'A weakening.'

'Why have you done this?' she asked softly.

'When I discovered you were going home needlessly,
but were still stubbornly refusing to listen to what my
heart was telling you, I thought a romantic gesture might
melt your hard heart.'

'Oh Matt!' It *had* melted. Molten, swirling in a heated
mass, raising her blood-pressure dangerously. It was the
most wonderful, stupid, ridiculous, romantic gesture that
she could ever have imagined.

'For an intelligent woman, you have a remarkably
limited vocabulary,' said Matt, his words cracking just a
little at the light in her eyes.

'You forgot the music,' she chided gently.

'No, I didn't. Listen.'

Eve tilted her head to one side. There was the sound of
the waves, lapping the beach softly, a deep whirring from
the cicadas and a perfect stillness in the air.

'Can't you hear the stars whispering?' asked Matt.
'They're reminding me that mermaids must always eat
their last course in the sea. Up you get, and over here.'

'I couldn't eat anything,' she protested, as he led her by
the hand to the water's edge.

'Only a little warm flesh,' he promised, drawing her
into the gently lapping waves.

'Matt, no further . . .'

'Why not?' They were waist-deep now, her dress
floating around her like a petal.

'I . . . We've just eaten!'

'Eve! There's no danger,' he chided softly. 'Well,' he

amended, with wide, innocent eyes. 'Not *much*.'

His hands reached for the buttons which ran down the front of her dress, shrugging it from her shoulders in a practised gesture, then disposing of her lacy bra, throwing both on to the beach. With some difficulty, he removed his own shirt, his fingers unable to obey with sufficent agility because Eve's hands were wonderingly exploring each fine laughter-thread that ran from the corner of his gleaming tawny eyes.

'That's enough,' he grated, pulling her deeper into the water. She felt her breasts rise, lifting in the gently moving waves, and her gaze flew from them to his heavily rising chest, glass-brown and glittering wet.

'I thought of making a huge notice which said "Eve Foster I love you signed Matt Cavell", but decided against it,' he said shakily. 'I couldn't find enough sheets to stretch across the bay.'

'I'm relieved to hear it,' she whispered.

'There are some fish, doing a fly-past, or rather a swim-under, somewhere out there,' he said with a straight face, pointing vaguely out to sea. 'I thought you'd like to know.'

'Original,' she giggled.

'I'm waiting,' he said ominously.

She raised her eyebrows in query.

'The words, woman. I've worked all afternoon on those damn baby chickens and I want some return.'

'You mean, "thank you"?' she asked innocently.

At his muttered curse, she laughed softly. His fingers stole treacherously to her breasts, gently persuading them to swell under his touch. As his mouth surrounded one nipple, where it lay just on the surface of the water, she moaned quietly at the upsurge of tiny pains which drove her hips to thrust against his in urgent demand.

'I want you to tell me that you believe in my love, that you trust me and will marry me. We'll work together Eve, be together always. You'll find our work so rewarding. And I want you to say that you're going to begin right now to think up the stories you're going to tell our children. Will you tell them about croaking butterflies?' he smiled. 'And me, I want to hear them, too.'

'No, I won't,' she said, shaking her head.

'*Whaaat*!' His yell echoed across the sea.

'Oh, I never repeat stories,' she said with a gurgle. 'I'd have to work on something new, like a bridge with hiccups, or . . .'

'For an intelligent woman,' he said tenderly, 'you talk too much. Close your mouth. No! Open it. Open it, say you love me, and keep it open. There are things I must do with it.'

Eve's laughing eyes looked into the sweet desire of those twin golden demons which sparkled at her. 'I love you,' she said demurely.

'That'll do for the moment, don't say any more,' he murmured, his head dipping to claim her mouth.

At the heart-tugging love in her soul, Eve's breath constricted in her throat, and she gave a low, rough cry.

'What is it, my sweetheart?' asked Matt gently.

'Nothing,' she said, pressing her naked breasts against his trembling chest. 'Only a passing butterfly.'

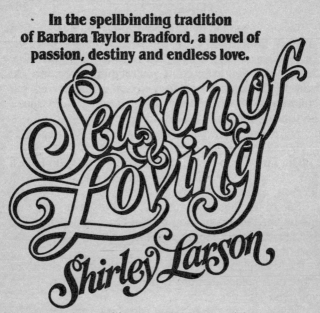
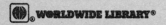

ATTRACTIVE, SPACE SAVING BOOK RACK

Display your most prized novels on this handsome and sturdy book rack. The hand-rubbed walnut finish will blend into your library decor with quiet elegance, providing a practical organizer for your favorite hard-or soft-covered books.

Only $9.95

Approximately 16" x 8" when assembled

Assembles in seconds!

To order, rush your name, address and zip code, along with a check or money order for $10.70* ($9.95 plus 75¢ postage and handling) payable to *Harlequin Reader Service*:

Harlequin Reader Service
Book Rack Offer
901 Fuhrmann Blvd.
P.O. Box 1396
Buffalo, NY 14269-1396

Offer not available in Canada.

BKR-1A

*New York and Iowa residents add appropriate sales tax.

PAMELA BROWNING

. . . is fireworks on the green at the Fourth of July and prayers said around the Thanksgiving table. It is the dream of freedom realized in thousands of small towns across this great nation.

But mostly, the Heartland is its people. People who care about and help one another. People who cherish traditional values and give to their children the greatest gift, the gift of love.

American Romance presents HEARTLAND, an emotional trilogy about people whose memories, hopes and dreams are bound up in the acres they farm.

HEARTLAND . . . the story of America.

Don't miss these heartfelt stories: American Romance #237 SIMPLE GIFTS (March), #241 FLY AWAY (April), and #245 HARVEST HOME (May).

HRT-1

◈ Harlequin Superromance

**Here are the longer, more involving stories you
have been waiting for... Superromance.**

Modern, believable novels of love, full of the complex
joys and heartaches of real people.

Intriguing conflicts based on today's constantly
changing life-styles.

Four new titles every month.
Available wherever paperbacks are sold.
